The Eridanos Library 12

Alexander Lernet-Holenia

The Resurrection
of Maltravers

Translated by
Joachim Neugroschel

Eridanos Press

Original German title *Die Auferstehung des Maltravers*

Copyright © 1984 by Paul Zsolnay Verlag, Vienna, Austria.

Translation Copyright © 1988 by Joachim Neugroschel.

Of the present edition Copyright © 1988
Eridanos Press, Inc., Hygiene, Colorado

Distributed in the U.S.A. by Rizzoli International
Publications, Inc., 597 Fifth Avenue, New York, NY 10017

Cloth: ISBN 0941419-22-3
Paper: ISBN 0941419-23-1
LC 88-80806

The Resurrection of Maltravers

ONE

Count Maltravers, after completing a prison sentence of twenty-two months, traveled from Pest to Jablonitz by way of Waitzen, Neuhäusl, and Sered. He crossed the border at Szob. He changed trains in Galanta. It began raining after Sered, but the rain soon stopped. Maltravers sat alone in the train compartment with his hat on his head and his hands in his lap. He was lean and of medium height, with a pale brown face; he was sixty-three years old.

He gazed through the window, but no one could have seen whether he really saw what he saw. However, a few minutes before Jablonitz, he stood up, pulled on his coat, stepped out into the corridor, and waited—like someone accustomed to waiting for specific times.

In Jablonitz, a man in green livery was standing on the station platform. Maltravers saw him and asked:

"From Sobotitz?"

"Yessir," the man in livery replied. He climbed into the train and took hold of two suitcases at which Maltravers pointed. Then the two men got out, and the train lumbered on.

The two men walked through the station.

"A footman?" asked Maltravers.

"No, your lordship," said the man in livery. "A gardener."

A game cart stood behind the station.

The driver, sitting on the driver's seat, a white-haired man with a large, blackened moustache, tipped his hat and said:

"I kiss your hand, young master!"

Maltravers, not giving him more than a fleeting glance, nodded and climbed into the cart. The suitcases were loaded, the gardener sat down next to the driver, and the cart took off.

At first, they drove along the Mjava, a dismal river, with muddy, gray-leafed willows drooping over the water; then they passed through two small villages. The wide, sandy road was only superficially moistened by the downpour. The cart turned to the left, Sobotitz emerged, they drove through the village. The rain had been heavier here, and a huge throng of geese wallowed about in the puddles. Behind the village, the estate rose out of treetops.

The cart pulled into an avenue lined with acacias, drove past farm buildings, turned into the courtyard, and stopped in front of the mansion.

The courtyard was empty, and drops of water showered down from the trees, in which a bluster of wind was caught.

Nor did anyone appear at the windows of the house. However, a footman was waiting at the entrance to receive him.

"Is my brother not here?" asked Maltravers.

"His lordship and her ladyship," said the footman,

"had to go to Hirschberg. In the meantime, I am to bring his lordship upstairs; his lordship is still at home and will be coming up himself."

He meant that he had been told to take Georg Maltravers into the house, and that Alexander Maltravers, the other one, would appear later.

Georg Maltravers got down from the cart, the gardener took hold of the suitcases again, and they followed the footman through the ground-level hall and up a stairway. They passed through a huge room with murals and a red marble floor, then up a gray stone staircase covered with a red velvet carpet and an ivory-colored linen runner. On the second landing, they walked down a long corridor filled with antlers and many greenish gold doors, one of which the footman opened. The two men stepped into a suite of relatively simple rooms. The windows of these rooms were open. The gardener put down the valises and withdrew. Glancing about, Maltravers tossed his gloves on the table; the footman helped him out of his coat. Finally, Maltravers took off his hat; one could now see that his head was shorn and covered with very little stubble that had grown in. He handed the footman the keys to the suitcases, and while they were being unpacked, the count walked over to the window, lit a cigarette, and gazed down into the garden.

A parterre, with a central fountain weeping over roses that were losing their petals, vanished toward the back into bushes and woody groves, and gigantic clouds of foliage hung, even from the sides, over the mossy brick paths.

The fountain, grayish silver, gushed and gushed, brimming over at the top like a willow; and a swift blackbird whisked through the grass. It was only when a puff of wind got caught in the jet of water that the

5

silver haze fell upon the lawn, so that nothing could be heard, and the blackbird evaded the squirting. Then the drops fell back into the basin, sounding like tears falling into a silver bowl.

Twilight set in.

Tossing the cigarette down into the garden, Maltravers turned away and leaned against the windowsill for a while. Eventually, he began to help the footman unpack. The valises were filled with nothing but old things, worn-out suits and defective linen, but meticulously overhauled and also folded and arranged with careful discipline, like the belongings of soldiers in barracks. Maltravers attentively watched the footman distribute everything in the closets.

However, the footman was not quite done when Alexander Maltravers entered the room and switched on the light.

He was slightly older than his brother. Looking at him for a moment, he then walked over and held out his hand.

"How are you?"

"Fine, thank you," said Georg Maltravers. "And you?"

"We have been invited to dinner in Hirschberg," said Alexander Maltravers, "and we could not beg off. Cecile and the children have gone on ahead, but I was waiting for you, and I am now going to join them. Please forgive us for leaving you alone on your very first evening."

"Think nothing of it," said Georg Maltravers.

Hirschberg was the home of the Duke de Joyeuse, an emigré and a prince of royal blood. Cecile was Alexander Maltravers's wife. The "children" were two old maids. The son, younger than his sisters, was in England, looking for an heiress to marry.

6

"May I have them bring you tea?" asked Alexander Maltravers.

"No thank you," said Georg Maltravers. "I will presently be having supper anyway, and I will then go to bed. In any case, I am very grateful to you for allowing me to stay here—"

"Why, but that's natural," said Alexander Maltravers, "that's natural!" There was a pause; then he added: "By the way, we've got the suitcases with the things you sent over from Skalitz back then. Should I have them brought up?"

"I will go through them tomorrow," said Georg Maltravers.

Skalitz was a vast estate, several hours away; he had lost it. At the time, he had sent over a few personal items. That was twenty years ago. He had never gone home again.

The brothers stood there for a few moments; finally, Georg Maltravers shrugged.

"Well," said Alexander Maltravers, "I have to leave now. *Auf Wiedersehen.*"

"*Auf Wiedersehen,*" said Georg Maltravers. "And please give my very best to Cecile!"

"Thank you," said Alexander Maltravers and left.

A short time later, the footman left too.

Georg Maltravers dined below, in the small salon, at eight P.M. Then he spent an hour sitting in the library and smoking. At nine–thirty, he went to bed. But he could not sleep; the solitude frightened him. He did not drop off until around two in the morning, when he heard the carriages returning.

He woke up at six and had to figure out where he was, but then he fell asleep again. Toward noon, he went downstairs, but was told that the count and countess had gone hunting in Jeschnitz, and that he was to eat alone again. He took advantage of his sister-in-law's absence to leave her a calling-card, for he couldn't stand her. He then spent the afternoon going through the contents of the valises from Skalitz. They contained nothing but old, rotten stuff—uniforms, box coats, foot muffs, and the like. But that evening, when he was told that the family would once again not be dining, they were too tired and had already gone to bed, Maltravers walked right into the estate office, where, as it turned out, his brother was still working. With a glance, Georg Maltravers dismissed the administrator.

"Listen," he said, "I fully realize that you personally would not leave me alone, you are doing it only because your wife wishes it. But I must confess that I do not wish to see Mistress Meyer either" (meaning Cecile, née Baroness Meyer-Waldeck). "Granted, I would have put up with her for your sake. But that is now superfluous. And indeed, I never cared for her. I can forgive such people for having money. It is my Christian duty to forgive them, even when they use it to such dreadful ends. For example, having one of their daughters marry you. But when commoners have so little self-regard as to force their way into the aristocracy, then I cannot forgive them. After all, one is what one is. There is no other nobility. And a person may come down in the world, but never up. Tell that to your wife! The disastrous thing about snobbery is that snobs not only are cretins, but they cretinize the people to whom they would like to climb up. You have become as big a cretin as your wife. I can accept rejection from anyone, but not from people who reject me purely because they have the right to do so, just as you people, for example, have a right to reject me. From now on, I will take my meals in my room!"

And before Alexander Maltravers could so much as

defend himself or his wife, Georg Maltravers stormed out, slamming the green padded door behind him.

From then on, he spent his days roaming the countryside. It was a very warm autumn, 1932. He usually took along a shotgun and fired at crows and jays, or else he stretched out in a haystack, watching the farmhands at work. He decided that the Slovakian girls had far smaller calves than during his youth. In the evening, he would sit in the library, trying to read, but he could never get himself to touch a book. He then wandered aimlessly around the house, and the family had their hands full trying to avoid running into him. For when he entered a room, he paid increasingly less heed to whether there was anyone present who did not care to see him. Instead, the others had to comply with him. Baroness Meyer-Waldeck in particular found him dreadful, and eventually she kept to her room altogether. He himself indulged more and more in reveries. Something began to happen inside him, something very different than in his earlier life. He now seldom fired at birds; the important thing for him was to have the ejectors release the empty shells whenever he opened the fowling piece. He loved watching the shells leap out, and if no birds were around, he would fire at random after aiming pensively for a long time.

It was on such an occasion, roughly in mid-October, that one of the two barrels burst, perhaps because of an error in the construction or perhaps because the mouth had clogged up when he had been heedlessly lying in a haystack. In any event, the barrel exploded, injuring his left hand, not seriously, but causing a great loss of blood. He wrapped a handkerchief around his hand and tried to get home, but after several hundred feet, he blacked out. A peasant lifted him up, placed him on his wagon, and took him home, like the peasant in the tale of Sir Lancelot of the Lake.

Maltravers soon came to, and his wound was tended by a physician. But, weakened by the loss of blood, the count stayed in bed for two days. The fever that had set in went down soon. Alexander Maltravers visited him daily. But on the third day, when Georg Maltravers wanted to get up, he could not quite resolve to do so. Instead, he remained lying, as he did on the fourth day; and on the fifth day his fever returned, although the wound was healing quickly.

The physician had told him to get up, but he stayed in bed, lying on his back with his eyes shut, eating cinchona; and if the windows were open during the afternoon, he would listen to the slightest swishing of the fountain, which sounded as if someone were weeping in the garden. He felt very tired. He was visited not only by Alexander Maltravers, but also by the latter's two daughters, the old maids, and they interfered with his listening to the fountain. Toward the end of the month, his fever went up, his ribs hurt, he was given injections twice, and one day, Cecile Maltravers appeared at his bed.

Since his indifference to his surroundings had kept increasing without his realizing it, it took him several minutes to fully grasp that "Mistress Meyer" was here. But then he instantly told himself that if she had come, he must be very ill. For otherwise, he assumed, she would not have come.

He sat up from his reclining position, refused to listen to her apparently sympathetic words, and vehemently commanded that his brother should come. Alexander Maltravers entered the room, and Georg Maltravers, suddenly almost shouting, demanded to know what was wrong with him.

Nothing, nothing, said Alexander Maltravers, he was just running a slight temperature. But Georg Maltravers yelled that it was not true, he was very ill, but they were keeping the truth from him, and they were doing nothing, so that he would die and they would be rid of him. The doctor was to come immediately!

However, the doctor also simply calmed him down, gave him another injection, and said it was nothing serious, so that Georg Maltravers demanded that they summon another physician immediately from Bratislava. But after the second physican arrived and examined him, he too merely said reassuring and evasive things, whereupon Maltravers told himself that he was doomed.

All night long, he wrestled with his fear of death. The wound in his hand had cleared up; that could not be the cause of his malady. He must have developed pneumonia from lying in bed for such a long time, or else it was old age, or just simply death coming, death!

He did not recall that he had ever feared death, but now that he was about to die, his fear was immeasurable. This fear, which he had always scorned and which had never dared to approach him, was now getting back at him. If it had been unable to keep his life easy and risk-free, it now at least made his death hard. He suffered the complete collapse of a hero—however dubious and disreputable, but still a hero. Had he not been so courageous earlier, he could not have been so cowardly now that his nerves were failing him. For it is the scope of one's courage that is important, and not the courage per se. However, at the crucial moment, the only truly decisive one, he was abandoned by everything: boldness, refinement, self-confidence, even self-esteem. All that remained was panic at the thought of death. He wracked his brain, trying to come up with ways of fleeing death. Suddenly, he reached a decision, asked for pen and paper, and wrote a confused letter to the Duke de Joyeuse in Hirschberg. He asked the duke to come to him, to apply the miraculous treatment of the royal house of France—and heal him by laying on his hands.

The duke came immediately, but explained that the only person who could cure him by laying on his hands was not he but the king himself, and only when he was "in a state of grace," that is, right after the coronation, and he could only treat scrofula, the king's evil, from which Maltravers was certainly not suffering. Besides, he went on, no king of France had been crowned for a long time now, and the pretender did not possess any supernatural faculties worth mentioning, so that the whole thing was simply out of the question. Maltravers could thank the Republic and the Bonapartes for that. However, if Maltravers wished, then he, Joyeuse, would remain and pray for the future salvation of Maltravers's soul. For like all truly religious people, he set no store, or not very much, by mere miracles.

Maltravers was desperate, but after lying motionless for almost fifteen minutes without answering, he sat up and scrawled a telegram to Monsieur de la Baume, a Hospitaller who lived in Prague. He asked him to come immediately.

The full name of this Knight of Malta was: Anne de la Baume le Boutillier d'Outremer. He had been christened Anne, albeit a female name, for reasons of tradition. The family had been given the epithet Le Boutillier d'Outremer during the crusades; it meant: "bottler from overseas," for certain members of this family had been granted the right to hang a canteen of water or wine from the saddle of the Grand Master of the Templars before they rode into the desert.

When Le Boutillier arrived and entered the dying man's room, he found not only Georg and Alexander Maltravers, Cecile, and the daughters, but also the Duke de Joyeuse together with his three natural sons: the Grand Bastard de Joyeuse, Count Eudes de Dampierre, and the Vidame Ghislain de Montrésor, as well as Montrésor's wife, Blanche, a tall, wonderful woman with dark blonde hair and bluish eyebrows. The priest was also present. It was a stately assembly, which had decided, at the duke's behest, to accompany Georg Maltravers's death with prayers. Not even Cecile Maltravers dared to stay away, although she did not believe in God.

"La Baume," the duke cried to the Hospitaller, "what do you say to this?"

"Your Royal Highness," replied La Baume, "I don't even know what's wrong!"

"Come here," ordered Georg Maltravers. "Come here immediately, Anna!" (He used the German form of the name.) And when the Hospitaller reached the bed, Maltravers told him to lay his hands on him and expel the illness.

"My goodness," La Baume exclaimed, "I didn't even know you were ill! What's the problem? And what should I lay on? My hands? Why?"

"The duke," Maltravers moaned, "did not want to."

"No," cried Joyeuse, "heaven forfend! *Ne plaise à Dieu!*"

"Perhaps he could not," murmured Maltravers. "But you," he said, staring at La Baume, "you can do it."

"I?"

"Yes, you, Anna!"

"Please do not call me Anna," said the Hospitaller, "otherwise I won't lay anything on you! My name is Anne! And why do you want something laid on you?"

13

"You people were always Knights of Malta," Maltravers moaned, "and before that you were Templars. The Templars had secrets; you know their secrets. You people can heal the sick. Lay your hands on me!"

"The Templars," said Joyeuse, "were heretics and sodomites. If they liked a nanny-goat, they would send her roses, and their donkeys had diamond bracelets. Those were their only secrets, and that was why good King Philip disbanded their order and had their Grand Master, Monsieur de Molay, burned at the stake. Isn't that so?" he asked the priest, while Le Boutillier made a face, glancing bitterly at the duke.

However, the priest, who had long forgotten who the Templars were, merely said unctuously: Whoever is destined to die must simply submit to God's will, and Maltravers should content himself with the consolations of the holy faith.

But Maltravers cursed and shouted that these consolations were no consolation if he could not go on living. Ever since the days of Fénélon, he cried, religion had been a matter of the mind and morality, but not a practical issue. He did not wish to die, and they would therefore have to resort to magic again, for he was convinced, he said, that his life was not over, his mind was teeming with plans, it was merely his wretched treatment at the hands of his family that was putting him into the grave, they simply wanted to get rid of him, but it would not work, the Hospitaller should lay his hands on him immediately. And the count's eyes darted from one person to another, imploring help, until they finally rested on Mme. de Montrésor, as if it were impossible to die in the presence of such great beauty. It occurred to him that the French royal family imagined that it descended from Troy, from Anchises and Aphro-

14

dite: Perhaps Mme. de Montrésor was a reincarnation of the goddess and was delighting in his mortality. . . .

"Listen," Boutillier said at last, "just what is it you want me to do? Lay my hands on you? Are you serious? You really think it will help?"

"Of course!" Maltravers begged. "Do it! For the love of God, Le Boutillier!"

Le Boutillier reflected for several moments, then agreed to do it. He asked the others to step outside. "He's crazy," he whispered to them, "but if he's really dying, why not do him the favor?"

Joyeuse felt one shouldn't fool around with such matters even in a case of death; the Templars had been utterly dubious sorts, as one could tell by, say, La Baume's first name. But then Joyeuse finally left the room with the others.

When the Hospitaller was alone with the patient, he sat down on the edge of his bed, and Maltravers grabbed Le Boutillier's hands, laying them on his own forehead and eyes. At that instant, Le Boutillier realized that Maltravers was dying. His reclining body jolted, and he sat up halfway. Le Boutillier hastily withdrew his hands from the patient's eyes, reached for a glass of port on the night table, and was about to hand it to him. But as he bent over, Maltravers sat further up, their heads collided, the port was spilled on the bed cover, Maltravers fell back and was dead.

Oddly enough, during these critical seconds, the Hospitaller had felt as if the eerie events were taking place not in front of him but in back of him, as if some ghostly being had appeared behind him, but had already left. The Knight of Malta looked around, but saw nothing. He placed the wine glass back on the night table and rubbed his forehead on the spot where it had bumped Maltravers's forehead; he then stood up, walked out, and told the others that Maltravers had died.

That was on the third of November, toward seven in the evening. The next morning, the corpse was washed by the gravedigger and his wife, and because no other imposing attire was found among Maltravers's belongings, he was dressed in an old militia lancer uniform that was in the valises from Skalitz. The dead man was then put in state in the small chapel next to the cemetery.

Cecile Maltravers said she was glad he was out of the house, for while she did not believe in ghosts, she considered it aristocratic to act as if she *were* afraid of them, and, furthermore, to insert a few words in consideration of St. Hubert's Day, which was spoiled by the death.

November 6 was the day of the funeral, and in the morning, Alexander Maltravers, accompanied by the gravedigger, appeared in front of the cemetery. He told the gravedigger, who had the keys, to unlock the door (which was locked every night), for he wanted to shut the coffin. The gravedigger unlocked the door and stepped aside, in order to let the count enter first. But no sooner had the count opened the door than he slammed it shut, as if deeply shaken, leaned momentarily on the door, in utter bewilderment, suddenly grabbed the key from the gravedigger's hands, locked the door, thrust the key into his own pocket, and said he had to go back home, he had forgotten something, and he would return later. But, to the gravedigger's amazement, the count did not head straight home. Instead, muttering to himself, he ran several times around the chapel and the cemetery and also through the cemetery until he finally vanished in the direction

16

of the manor house. At home, he instantly dashed into his dead brother's room, locked himself inside for a quarter of an hour, and fumbled around in his brother's belongings, yanking and slamming the closet doors, whereupon, clutching a cavalry saber with its sheath, he dashed out of the house and over to the chapel, opened the door, entered without the gravedigger, and locked himself in again. Hammer thuds were then heard, he was obviously nailing the coffin shut without witnesses—an utterly improper action. But, the count being a count, the gravedigger did not have the nerve to object. When Alexander Maltravers left the chapel again, the coffin was indeed shut, the pall was covering it, and a saber, czapka, and cartridge were arranged picturesquely on the coffin. The count told the gravedigger—who, by now, viewed the count's activities as very eerie—that he had had to go back for his brother's saber, which he had forgotten to bring along. However, the gravedigger clearly remembered that he had brought the saber to the chapel two days ago, along with the other objects and the pall.

Be that as it may, the funeral took place at two–thirty that afternoon in pouring rain. The duke, his sons, and the Knight of Malta were also present, as well as many people from the village and even a few neighboring landowners. For once a person is dead, people refrain from totting up his deeds and misdeeds. Otherwise, how many unpaid accounts would be settled! Because of the rain, the peasant women held their smocks over their heads and stood in their petticoats, while Monseigneur, the duke, gazed pensively at their calves. Cecile Maltravers, however, wept and ordered her daughters to weep, which was not difficult, since the band was way off key. After the service, the duke, his sons, Madame de Montrésor, and the landowners

17

stayed on for tea, which lasted until late at night, with everyone getting fairly intoxicated, so that they all retained a lovely memory of Maltravers's death. However, the Knight of Malta, preferring to avoid this sort of funeral feast, had already departed.

Actually, however, they had not laid Georg Maltravers to rest. Rather, they had buried an empty coffin containing several bricks, which had been carefully lodged between the sawdust and the pillows so that the bricks would not rumble about.

TWO

When the gravedigger had opened the door for him, Alexander Maltravers had instantly seen that his brother was no longer lying in the coffin. Instead, the coffin, half capsized, lay empty on the floor, and Georg Maltravers was nowhere to be found in the chapel. For a country nobleman, Maltravers was very quick in reaching his decision not to raise a fuss whatever may have occurred, or at least to conceal the matter from the gravedigger. However, given all the trouble that his brother had caused during his lifetime, Alexander Maltravers may have been mentally prepared to suffer one of his pranks after his death. In any case, the first thing he did was to slam the chapel door and lock it. Then, fearing a scandal that would crown all the previous events, he leaned, genuinely shaken, against the door and reflected lightning-fast: No one could possibly have stolen the corpse; it was not an object of value. He must therefore have regained consciousness and left the chapel on his own strength. But how? Not through the door. It had been locked. Ergo: through a window.

Murmuring that he had forgotten some of the "corpse accessories," the count hurried away from the gravedigger and ran around the chapel. All the windows had been left open because of the corpse, and the count noticed that one of the screens had been twisted up at one end, so that his resurrected brother must have squeezed through the aperture. Moreover, in the soft soil under the window, he discovered the fairly deep imprint left by his jump.

Georg Maltravers had not reappeared at the house, so he must have fainted en route or died a second time—whether definitively was still up in the air. In any case, Alexander Maltravers had no more confidence in his brother's death. He ran around the graveyard and across it, but did not find him lying anywhere; so he ran back to the house and up to his brother's room.

There, the lancer uniform in which he had been put in state was lying on the floor, soaked through, for it had rained that night; and next to it lay the saber.

At first, Alexander Maltravers could not figure out why his brother had taken along the saber, but then he soon found it, covered with soil and road mud at the lower end of the sheath. Evidently, the resurrected man had used it as a cane, to support himself in his weakness.

However, the count could still not ascertain his brother's whereabouts. But Georg Maltravers had pulled open the closet doors, which along with other evidence, such as the uniform on the floor, led Alexander Maltravers to conclude that his brother must have changed clothes. He had obviously been cold, for the windows of the death room, which had been open, were now shut.

Altogether, it was almost incomprehensible that,

after a serious case of pneumonia, from which, strictly speaking, he had not recovered, and after two days of lying in state in the cold, such an old man could have mustered the strength to return, change clothes, and disappear again. Nor could Alexander Maltravers explain where his brother might have entered the house. In any case, not through the front door, which had been locked. Perhaps through a window or a back door. Or did he have accomplices who had opened the door for him but concealed his reappearance? At any rate, the whole manner of his removal seemed to indicate that Georg Maltravers had wanted to keep his resurrection a secret. He may have reckoned on tacit approval and even assistance from his brother, who had no interest in his further presence and every interest in his disappearance, however it might occur. Georg Maltravers had come back to life, returned to the house, and then taken off, but wished to be regarded as dead.

Alexander Maltravers warmed up to this notion as soon as it struck him. Nor did he delve into any further particulars. He carefully hid the wet uniform, cleaned the dirt off the saber, took it over to the chapel, filled the coffin with bricks (which were piled up in a corner, probably ever since some repairs had been done to the chapel), and nailed up the coffin. In case anyone subsequently objected to the unreliability of this procedure without witnesses, he would certainly be able to hush it up with the sovereignty of a major landowner in such a remote area.

Finally, he had the coffin buried.

Of course, for days and weeks on end, he trembled at the thought that the whole business might come out and he would be reminded of his brother in a far more scandalous way than he had been accustomed to during his brother's lifetime. And he was alone with his worries, for he confided his secret in no one, not even his wife. However, he heard nothing from that brother of his, until he was notified much later that a man named Georg Fortescue had died in Venice. But Alexander Maltravers did not make a fuss about the news.

The night before the funeral, Georg Maltravers had regained consciousness around two or two–thirty A.M. He assumed he had merely been sleeping, and he felt cold and numb, but still thoroughly revitalized. He wanted to turn over in his bed, but went toppling down with the coffin, smashing so hard into the stone floor of the chapel that he saw stars.

For a while, he lay motionless with astonishment at the apparently enormous changes in his bedroom. Only Cecile Maltravers, he thought to himself, could have caused them. Moreover, it was dark and very cold, and somewhere the rain was gushing.

Eventually, he assumed that he had merely fallen out of bed; he stood up, wanting to switch on the light, but did not find any lamp. He also noticed that he was wearing strangely tight and unfamiliar clothes. Nor could he explain why he had been sleeping in them. Still, he scoured his pockets for matches, but found none. He groped about, and the spurs began to jingle on his boots. This confused him totally; he thought he had gone crazy. For an instant, he even believed he had died, and that this state was simply death. But all at once, he knocked over a large candelabra, felt along the floor in order to discover what he had knocked over, and found a box of matches, which had been lying in the bowl of the candlestick. He struck a match, saw the candelabra, set it up, lit the candle, and discovered his dreadful predicament.

That is to say, at first he was not surprised to be in the

chapel. For, prior to awakening, he had, oddly enough, dreamt that he was in a chapel. But then he saw that he was wearing one of his old uniforms and that a coffin was lying on the floor: the truth dawned on him. He was terrified. Cold sweat beaded on his forehead when he realized he could have been buried alive. Then he heaved a sigh of relief that it had not happened and that he had come to in the nick of time. He went to the door, found it locked, shook it and yelled, but everything remained silent, and no one opened.

A sudden weakness made his knees buckle; he walked back, sat down next to the toppled coffin, and realized that if he remained there until someone opened the door, that is, until morning, he would catch a chill. In general, he was at a loss to explain how he had survived his apparent death, although he had been lying in state in the cold. He did not know how long he had been lying there; he figured it must have been a day and at least half a night. Actually, it had been two days and almost two nights. However, he decided that he had come to again and noticed nothing of his illness but a great weakness, because the Knight of Malta had laid his hands on him. His action had certainly worked, albeit with much delay: the count had awoken to life again, and not really been dead all that time. But his brother's family had used this chance to get rid of him. After all, Cecile Maltravers would not have cared whether he was buried dead or alive. He also angrily noted that "Mistress Meyer" had provided very old, patched-up, threadbare linen for the coffin. He kicked it scornfully. He delighted in picturing how horrified Cecile would be by his resurrection. And he felt that he had been thrust into his uniform in a very sloppy, casual manner. His stockings, which were not pulled all the way up inside his boots, were scrunched up, chafing him, and a couple of buttons of the ulanka had not even been closed on his belly. He resolved to do everything in his power not to catch cold, not to die again, for he was so furious at his family that he wanted to punish them by remaining a burden on them for a long, long time.

Yet oddly enough, he almost yearned for death or what had seemed like death. In some inexplicable way, it had been a solace, almost a comfort, however much he may once have feared it. But now it was over. Everything passes, even, so it seemed, death. He was alive again and he decided to defy his family by remaining alive for a very long time.

Feeling cold, he wrapped himself in the velvet pall and sat, all bundled up, on the edge of the coffin, like a sick monkey. He was hungry and felt like smoking, at least—no doubt, partly to while away the time. But he found no cigarettes in his pockets. None had been put there, of course; it had not mattered to his family whether he would have anything to smoke in the eternal life.

He stared into space, wrapping himself up more snugly in the pall. A coat-of-arms was embroidered into each of its four corners: under a velvet hat encircled by a wreath of strawberry leaves, a blue shield strewn with golden toads and held by two winged stags, the whole thing draped in an ermine cloak; underneath it, a ribbon with the device: *Ressuscite, Fortescue!* Rise Up, or Arise from the Dead, Fortescue.

This was what it was all about:

Legend had it that the Maltraverses were ultimately descended from no lesser a being than Merowech, the son of an ocean demon, who had overpowered the Queen of the Franks as she bathed in the sea. When the Carolingians seized power in France (the Merowingians were said to be so incapable of maintaining the regency that, purely for prestige purposes, they had simply driven around the country in two-wheeled oxcarts, the kind used during the migration of the peoples)—when the Carolingians seized the throne, some of the last Merowingians fled to Norman territory, from where they upheld their hereditary claims. They continued to bear the most ancient French coat-of-arms, the golden toads, which eventually evolved into the lilies. The dukes of Normandy enfeoffed them with the Comté of Maltravers. The "heirs of the toads" recovered from the decay of their house and soon became such a powerful shield for the dukes of Normandy that they were surnamed "Fortescue," for "Fortescue" means "powerful shield." And their motto was: Arise and Take Your Inheritance!

They never did. But when the Normans conquered England, the Fortescue-Maltraverses went along, and they received County Surrey before it was given to the Howards. Eventually, they lost Comté de Maltravers in northern France, and it passed into the hands of the Sommerstorffs, a family from Cleve. Around the time of the Turkish Wars, a certain Hugh Fortescue-Maltravers, a younger son of the dynasty, arrived in Hungary, joined the fight against the Turks, became a general, and was made a count of *ancienne noblesse* by the Emperor, but without the predicate of "illustrious," for the other families protested, even though they themselves bore that title more or less illegitimately. However, the Emperor presented him with several estates in northern Hungary, including Skalitz and Sobotitz.

Georg Maltravers gazed and gazed at the device: Arise, Fortescue! Then he reached a decision.

He had died as a Maltravers, with a sullied reputation. He could arise as a Fortescue, with the immaculate honor of a newborn babe. He could not even be accused of misrepresentation if he assumed the name of Fortescue. When issuing a new passport to him after the war, the official had asked him his name, and the count had given his full name, "his grand old name of a gentleman": Georg Hugh Fortescue Count von Maltravers. This sort of thing no longer existed, the official had said. Titles had been abolished in Bohemia, Moravia, and Slovakia. Georg Fortescue was enough. And that was what the official wrote in the passport. However, the name of Fortescue was practically unknown. The family still went exclusively by the name of Maltravers.

Arise, Fortescue!

Maltravers arose, dropping the pall, went over to one of the high sills, and examined the window. Then, with great effort because of his feebleness, he piled several prayer desks under the window, took the saber lying next to the coffin, clambered up the desks, reached the window after several futile attempts, squeezed through the screen, and jumped out into the open.

His knees buckled so sharply that he almost collapsed. But he straightened up and, leaning on his saber, he headed toward Sobotitz in the pouring rain. His spurs jingled, but he soon tore them off his heels and threw them away.

He encountered no one.

He realized he could not possibly enter the house through the portal, which was bound to be locked. However, he recalled a tiny back door leading to the servants' quarters. In his youth, he had frequently depended on it when sneaking out of the house for his final nocturnal adventures with the Slovakian girls, who had at the time very thick calves. Often, he had gone with his boyhood friend, the now likewise old and white-haired coachman. This door had never closed properly; one only had to give it a hard yank to open it or to slam it shut so that it appeared to be locked.

When Maltravers reached this door and shook it, it opened as easily as ever. It had gotten no better. These locks never get better, he mused; at most, they get worse.

Just as he was entering, the clock in the gable of the house struck four with a tone distorted by the rain. He felt as if the house wanted to hold him up by signaling the sleepers. But he would not be held up.

He groped quietly through the darkness, came to his room, closed the windows, and slipped out of his uniform. Then he donned a suit and a coat, pocketing his passport and what little money he possessed. He happened to glance into a mirror. He looked wretched, his face had not been shaved for days. They may have shaved him, but his beard had kept growing after his death. He remembered being told that the hair of corpses in dry tombs often keeps growing several inches, sometimes even several feet. He was overwhelmed by a sense of the eerie, almost indecent fertility of death. Perhaps there was no real death. There was merely a different kind of life.

He put on his hat, grabbed a cane, and stole out of the house again. He almost regretted not encountering anyone, say Mistress Meyer-Waldeck; he would have had a chance to teach her to believe in ghosts.

Closing the back door behind him, he set out toward the nearest village.

It made no difference to him whether the family believed that he was dead or not or that he had vanished into thin air. He was fed up with them.

27

He trudged along so slowly that it was twilight by the time he arrived in the next village, where no one knew him anymore because he had not been in that area for years.

Renting a wagon from a peasant, he drove to the railroad station.

He took the direct train to Prague.

Exhausted, he slept almost all the way. But he no longer felt ill. He was cured, he thought to himself, because the Hospitaller had laid his hands on him.

When he arrived in Prague, which is also known as Golden Prague, it was already evening. He drove straight to the home of the Knight of Malta.

The Knight was not there; he was still at Maltravers's funeral, or rather en route back to Prague.

Maltravers told the butler that he was Count Fortescue and had been invited by the Hospitaller to spend a few days here.

Then he lay down right in the Hospitaller's bed.

When Anne de la Baume arrived the next morning, his butler informed him that Count Fortescue was already here.

Who? asked the Knight of Malta. Who was here?

Count Fortescue.

Who was that?

The gentleman lying inside in the bed.

"In the bed!" cried the Hospitaller. "Which bed? Mine?"

"Yes, My Lord."

The Knight of Malta dashed into his bedroom, and found Maltravers waking up in his bed after a sound sleep.

The Knight thought he had lost his mind.

"Good morning, Anna!" said Maltravers.

"My God!" stuttered the Knight. "What are you

doing here? You're dead! We buried you just yesterday!" And since his knees refused to obey him, he collapsed on the edge of a chair.

Maltravers asked the butler, who had reeled in behind his master, to serve breakfast. The guest then turned to Le Boutillier and said:

"You people buried me? Well, well. Fancy that. I hope it was at least a first-class funeral. How greatly the living honor themselves with the dead! However, I am not dead, to say the least. I may have been, but even that no longer strikes me as quite probable. For what, after all, is death and what is life? They are forms of intuition of one and the same state, nothing more. In any case, you cured me by laying on your hands—a bit late, to be sure, but still and all, it worked. Granted, I almost regret no longer being dead, so to speak, for it was really quite nice. But now I am alive again, and I owe it all to you, dear Anna!"

"Me?"

"Yes, you laid on your hands."

"Oh, go on! That's nonsense!"

"Do not say that. You are too modest. Or do you believe that one can lay hands on oneself?"

"What are you talking about?"

"I mean: Could I have brought myself back to life? It might very well be. Do you recall: I took your hands myself and placed them on me? My hands lay on yours as yours lay on my forehead. Perhaps my hands were more effective than yours. For we were healing people in France before the Capets arrived and began healing. And they are probably just our younger line anyway, the Christian *branche cadette* of the most pagan house of the Franks. I have never paid any attention to the nonsense of our lineage, but now I find that there may be some truth to it after all. So if you do not believe you may claim the honor of having resurrected me, then I myself managed to do so. But you can still think about it, Anna, if you prefer a different version."

"Let's forget about this resurrection!" shouted the Knight of Malta. "Just tell me how you came here? And why to *my* home, for God's sake?"

"Because," said Maltravers, "I trust you." And while breakfasting, he told him the entire story of his resurrection. A delicate scent of tea and the Hospitaller's West Indian rum drifted through the room as Maltravers revealed the secrets of his death to his friend. Meanwhile, he kept smearing butter on slices of toasted bread, shaking an enormous amount of salt on top, evidently in order to make up for the body salts that he had lost in the perspiration of death. The Hospitaller, still wearing his coat and hat, listened with gaping eyes. He was also still too bewildered to complain that Maltravers kept calling him "Anna."

"But you fell back," the knight kept repeating, "and you were dead."

"Not a jot!" said Maltravers. "When did I fall back?"

"When I was handing you the port wine."

"I did not fall back."

"You did so!"

"No. Our heads collided, and I told you to be careful."

"You did not say that. You had already died."

"That is not true," said Maltravers, "not true at all!" How could I have died if I drank up the port wine!"

"You did not drink it. It splashed on your bed cover, while you fell back and died."

Maltravers gazed at him thoughtfully. "Perhaps," he finally said, "perhaps it only seemed that way to you, Anna. But it seemed to me that I got out of bed and said that the laying-on of your hands had been very useful, I was now healthy, but I was fed up with my family, and I wanted to go to Paris."

"Paris?"

"Yes."

"The very idea!"

"Not a bad one. And I intend to carry it out."

"But, my goodness," cried the Hospitaller, "what was it like when you were dead and fancied you weren't dead?"

"Very nice, I already told you. But do not imagine that I am going to reveal the secrets of death to you, my good Anna. Secrets cannot be revealed. They have to be experienced—even if it kills you. In short, after getting out of bed, I wanted to have a bath and a shave. Then I dressed and informed my brother that I would be leaving for Paris that same evening, for I really wanted nothing more to do with him and Cecile, and I told him to give me a wagon and get me to the railroad station. I also asked him for money. He gave me some without making a great to-do."

"Wishful thinking!" cried the Hospitaller.

"Perhaps. But I will now ask you for some."

"What? Money?"

"Yes indeed."

The Knight of Malta gestured vaguely.

"Well, anyway," Maltravers went on, "my brother gave me the money, and I packed my things, took leave of all of you very hastily. You, dear Anna, were the only one to whom I said goodbye very cordially, and then I climbed into the wagon, which was standing in the courtyard. All the windows in the house were lit up, and from every window many faces looked down at me, your faces were among them as well as numerous unfamiliar ones. But I climbed into the wagon, and we drove to the station. That is, we intended to drive to the station, but we did not get there."

"How come?"

"We went astray in the darkness. The driver was a jackass. We lost our way, and all at once we found ourselves in a vast forest. It was the forest that stretched toward the mountains. It was very dense and dark. I told the driver to head south, not north. He replied that he *was* driving south, but he nevertheless kept going north. The trees in the forest were huge, and the foliage, if they still had any, dangled right into us. We kept driving along bumpy wheel tracks and over tree roots, and then we came into a hollow and turned into another one, and then suddenly we found ourselves in a whole labyrinth of deep hollows, with leaves and wild grapes drooping into them; they were covered with cobwebs and banged into our faces. It was also raining all the time and pitch-black, and the hollows sank deeper and deeper into the ground. Finally, at a crossing of two hollows, I forced the driver to turn back, but we still had a long way to go. We also forded a river, and the water reached up to the hubs of our wheels. I did not know this river. But in the distance, we heard the roar of other rivers, as if they were plunging through chasms. By the time we finally emerged from the forest, it was already two A.M. We found ourselves near the chapel of the cemetery. I told the driver I would not be able to catch any train, but I did not want to return to Sobotitz either, so I would spend the night in the chapel. I entered the chapel, wrapped myself up in my coat, lay down on the floor, and fell asleep. I had pleasant dreams. I do not precisely recall what I dreamt, but for a while I felt a rocking, as if I were lying in a ship.

When I awoke, I wanted to turn over, but then I crashed down from the bier with the entire coffin. I lit a candle and saw what had happened."

Le Boutillier had listened, shaking his head, and he then said:

"But you must have noticed in your way that you were washed, shaved, and dressed by the gravedigger and his wife, taken to the chapel, and put in state."

"Possibly." said Maltravers. "Now I want to spend a few days here, to recover."

"In my bed?"

"Yes indeed. Had you been pious enough to spend another day or two in Sobotitz and take part in my funeral feast, you would not have come home until tomorrow or the day after. But now, you can sleep on your couch for the time being. And you must not tell anyone that I am still alive and that I am here. Do you understand, Anna?"

"Stop calling me Anna," the Knight of Malta shrieked. "You know I can't stand it. You are to call me Anne."

"Oh, please!" said Maltravers. "It is not important. The important thing is that I am asking you to lend me money, for it was you, after all, who brought me back to life, and you are therefore obligated to take care of me for now. I want to get a new wardrobe and then go to Paris."

"And what do you intend to do there? Live it up perhaps?"

"I am not sure. In any case, the life that has been granted me anew is now in the hands of the Almighty. It calms my mind to know that I owe it to divine providence and not to the carelessness of a married couple. Providence certainly intended to resurrect me; and even before my death, I sensed that I still had things to do. That is why I did not want to die. I am certain that something lies ahead for me."

"Oh," murmured the Knight of Malta, "what can it possibly be! Another one of the ugly and immoral affairs that you always had in the past."

"No," said Maltravers, "not at all. From now on, I will only have very moral affairs."

"Don't make yourself look ridiculous in the bargain!" cried Le Boutillier.

"You," said Maltravers, "have no right whatsoever to suspect a good resolution. Did not God give you too— and with no intention whatsoever on your part—the strength to bring me back to life, even though your forebears committed all the atrocities of the Orient, Anne de la Baume!"

"I forbid you," shrieked La Baume, "to blab the fairy tales that Monseigneur has told and that he repeats only because they suit the French Royal House! Had you people remained kings instead of the Capets, you would probably have behaved a lot worse toward us, you Maltraverses!"

"Quite likely," said Maltravers perfunctorily. "Indeed, highly likely. In any event, you would have never found any occasion to criticize my moral stance. Morality usually takes last place anyway, and you can see that my life is not yet over. Until something ends, one cannot say whether it was moral or not. Many things that I have done and that, superficially considered, looked moral turned out eventually to be indecent, and very many of my alleged indecencies have ultimately proved moral. Not even I was able to make any precise forecast. So at least be so indulgent as to wait for the end, dear Anna!"

"No," snapped the Hospitaller and stood up. "Anna

will wait for nothing, nor does he care to have anything to do with the whole matter. Generally, people are delighted when someone is still alive instead of being dead, but this is not a serious business with you. It is just another of your usual pranks. You can recuperate here, for all I care, you can even have some money. And you don't need to pay me back. But once you can go, then go! And God help you!"

"Yes," said Maltravers, "God help me, for life is hard, and death was easy. I have not told you everything; it is very difficult to talk about it. But death was much easier than life. I shall never again be able to live so easily after being dead."

Two weeks later, he boarded the train for Paris. Leafing through one of the newspapers in his lap, he found an obituary for himself. It said more or less the following:

After an initially brilliant and then equally wretched life, Count Georg Maltravers, one of the last aristocratic adventurers of the nineteenth century, had passed away just a short while ago at the estate of his brother in Sobotitz. While still quite young, this second son of Count Ferdinand Maltravers had inherited several estates, including Skalitz, a small kingdom. However, he had abused the gifts granted him by nature and by the grace of destiny. After frequenting the most fashionable gathering-places of high society, including Vienna, Paris, and London, and dissipating not only his own inheritance but also the dowries from his two marriages, he had gotten into increasingly more dubious scrapes. For years, he had been renowned as the lover of hundreds of beautiful women and the hero of innumerable duels, a reputation that had gained him access to the highest circles. But eventually, the deceptive façade had collapsed, and he had been unmasked as a cardsharp, for which he had had to serve a prison

term of two years. A few short weeks after his return to
his brother's estate, an illness had terminated his life,
which, belonging to the questionable ideals of a past
era, had actually ended long ago.

Maltravers lowered the newspaper to his lap. "Oh,"
he murmured, "badly written! Bad and sentimental!
Cheap, demagogic falsehoods." But at the same time,
he felt that even a falsehood can, in an unsettling way,
be true, and gazing out the window, he recalled a few
lines by a Polish poet, whose name he had forgotten.
They kept repeating in his mind over and over again
with the rolling rhythm of the train:

> Will nothing grow from my life anymore,
> One year, or two, or x?
> Black swans of my thoughts galore
> Glide down the Vistula to the Styx.

THREE

In Paris one day, a Spanish broker named Gomez, who had once been a so-called *faiseur*, an intermediary in major financial transactions, but now had only a small agency, was told that a gentleman named Fortescue wished to see him, Georg Fortescue, a name that did not ring a bell. Nevertheless, he had the visitor shown in, while he kept leafing through the papers on his desk, evidently hunting for something specific. Eventually, he leaned over and began to comb through the side drawers of his desk. Meanwhile, Maltravers entered, and when the agent sat up and saw him standing before him, he thought it was a ghost.

"Count. . . . " he finally stuttered. "But count!"

"I am delighted to learn that the news of my demise has spread this far. Frankly, I no longer realized I was so famous in Paris as to believe that anyone here would take notice of my death."

"So then you didn't die," the agent stammered.

"As you can see," said Maltravers, sitting down on the

edge of an armchair and lighting a cigarette. "As you can see—or rather: I *did* die. But then I came back to life. Nonetheless, would you be so kind as not to tell anyone."

And he confided his story.

When Maltravers had finished, Gomez held his tongue. At last, he asked: "And is it true that you cheated at cards?"

"I must own up to it," said Maltravers.

"But how could you do that!" the agent exclaimed. "A man of your name and your standing! A figure greater than that of a Boni de Castellane!"

Maltravers smiled vaguely when he heard himself being compared with the famous adventurer.

"You are right," he said. "Really, how could I! One should never do anything that is not blameless. It is far more successful than impropriety. For no one expects it. But I no longer had the strength to act properly. Ah, had I only been young! But I was old and very tired; I wanted to make things easier for myself, so I cheated."

"And now?" asked Gomez after a pause. "What do you plan to do now?"

"Now," said Maltravers, "I wish to forget that I have already lived once."

"That," said the agent, "is one thing you should not do! Just think: a life like yours! Who else could have lived it in that way, who but you would have had the courage to live as Maltravers lived! You were one of the most courageous men I have ever known. . . ."

"When I was at death's door," murmured Maltravers, gazing blankly past the agent, "when I was really at death's door, I was a lot less courageous, my dear Gomez. You should have seen me! Yet I do not even reproach myself for having been afraid. On the contrary, despite my fear, I should have died courageously in order to be truly something like a hero. But I was no hero, God knows! An opportunity for bravery, encouraged for centuries by the bravery of a great house, a chance that usually does not recur—was shamefully squandered! However, I at least have the rare fortune of being able to die once again. Nevertheless, I will have to make a tremendous effort to snuff out the shame of my first death. For I behaved more miserably than even I would ever have expected, and the family of the Duke de Joyeuse was also, I believe, profoundly embarrassed by my want of restraint. Of course, those people take such things more lightly. After all, they have their absolute faith in heaven with its seven thousand saints, who await them by candlelight, quite aside from the roughly sixty to seventy saints that they have in their own family. But I should have had faith in myself. That would have been more. That would have simply been everything. However, I did not have that faith. And that was how I disgraced myself."

The agent looked at him. "I alone," he finally said, "once made a million from the boldness of your ventures."

"And where is it now, that million?" asked the count, peering around the shabby office.

"Bring me back Maltravers as he was, and I will earn that million again!"

"Ah," said the count, "Maltravers is dead; and in the netherworld, the shade of Boni de Castellane refuses to shake hands with the cardsharp. At a time when there were still lances, I would no doubt have been considered a mere *demie lance*. You will have to make do with a Fortescue, my dear Gomez. After all, you too are no longer the man you were. Anyway, we keep dying continuously. We lose more and more of the connection to everything we used to be. We yearn for it, but such yearning for the past is already death. Death is everything that was. I too now yearn for death, the way Lazarus, after his resurrection, is said to have yearned for his previous death. Supposedly, there was even considerable ill feeling between him and God's son. Eventually they both wept over that imprudent revival. And the pain caused by that blunder, even though he repeated it with several other people—including himself—the admission of that blunder contains the entire humanity of the Savior. For however deeply one loves life, one should love death more than life. Otherwise, one does not truly live life. One should get through it as a hero, not vegetate until the end, like a dog. But being resurrected is even worse. For how should one be able to live if one knows what death is like! I have to make a great effort to forget death. I must forget everything that was."

"And all your experience!" cried the broker, who was likewise old, but did not at all care to talk continuously about dying. "The tremendous experiences of a life such as yours?"

"Life," said Maltravers, "is not experience. True life is inexperience. If one wishes to live, one should have experienced nothing."

"My God," said Gomez, "how could you have lived after everything you've experienced! For example, did you absolutely have to go and cheat people at cards and then eventually be exposed like some raw beginner?"

"No," said Maltravers, "I did not have to. But one's mistakes are not due to clumsiness. One makes them simply because one wants to make them. We would be beggars if we could not even squander ourselves. But probably I just wanted to put an end to it."

"A fine end!"

40

"Yes, it was, because it was not an end. Evidently, I was despised even by death. However, ultimately, I too did not want to die. I suddenly felt as if I were planning something, but I do not know what, and I do not know how. . . . It was probably just fear. Fear of death. . . ."

"Oh, God," the agent cried nervously, "are you talking about death again? You never stop talking about it! You have a way of making conversation so neat and tidy that it could enervate a person, by God! Just don't be so melancholy! The very instant you walked in, I felt as if you smelled of tuberoses. In fact, a yearning for death is sweeping through Paris. Yesterday, for example, I took a cab, and the driver raced so furiously that I finally shouted at him, 'Ne filez pas comme ça!'—'Ah, m'sieur,' the man replied, 'ce matin ma femme m'a fait cocu. J'ne tiens plus à la vie. . . . ' However, I can no longer endure such things. Come on! Let's go out and have a drink somewhere. And I want to ponder whether anything can be done for you."

And seizing his hat, he took the count by the arm, and they left the office.

As they walked down the stairs, Maltravers remained silent. But once they came outdoors, he said, "Listen, Gomez, I must ask you something after all."

"Well?" said Gomez, heading toward a small café across the street.

"What kind of a person do you think I am?"

"What are you driving at?" asked Gomez, watching out for the vehicles as he steered through them. "What kind of a question is that?"

"I mean: We were acquainted in the past, and I have just paid you a quite noncommittal visit, purely for purposes of information. Now if you did not know me, or if you were to first meet me today, would you reject me too?"

41

"Oh, goodness," said Gomez, entering the café, "I have neither the time nor the occasion to deal with the morals of my clients. Morality is an issue for one's own conscience. Regarding you, I find that you were extremely clumsy. I have no right to say anything else." And, sitting down at a table, he ordered two aperitifs.

Maltravers stood next to the table for a moment, then sat down, saying: "Judging a person should be left up to the person himself. But people refuse to do so. The less right they have to condemn someone else, the more sharply they condemn him. Yet they would have the right to do so only if they had not done what they carp at others for doing. Indeed, usually they have not done so, but only because they did not have to, or because the opportunity did not present itself. In short, I find it repulsive that people who have never risked cheating or doing such things will impudently tell me that they will no longer associate with me. Instead, they ought to thank the Good Lord that it has not happened to them, for they are little people without courage. I would love to lure such people to walk on thin ice."

"Why?" asked Gomez. "What would you get out of it?"

"I would simply," said Maltravers, "like to place them in jeopardy. It does not take much skill to lead an unimpeachable life if one does not have the temperament to become disreputable. I hate people who are incapable of anything, good or bad. Only the man who has sinned a lot is forgiven a lot. But those who did not even have enough imagination to sin are forgiven nothing. They are lukewarm people. I could spend the rest of my life destroying their self-confidence."

"That," said Gomez absentmindedly, draining his glass, "would, of course, be sheer nonsense. Your victims might realize that it is not always so easy to be a man of honor. But what would *you* get out of it? We should really try to come up with something more sensible for you. And if, in addition, you can prove to the others that their lives are built on sand, then so much the better. For you can get a lot further with intimidated people than with those on a high horse. In any event, let me give it some thought."

He paid and they left.

Their conversation took place on a Wednesday. That Friday, Gomez had another meeting with Maltravers and set forth a project of a remarkable magnitude.

Several days later, the two men showed up at the training camp of Kid Harraden, who was preparing for his fight with Costenoble.

The camp was makeshift. A ring had been set up inside a large hall, and the spectators were sitting around it. But entire rows of seats were empty, for there was not much interest in the upcoming bout between Harraden and Costenoble.

Gomez and Maltravers settled on two of the empty seats.

In the ring, Harraden was busy warming up.

After a while, Harraden's manager, Josef Spiegel, came over, greeted Gomez, whom he already knew, and spoke a few words with him.

The gist of it was that the training camp had turned out to be a bad speculation, for the Parisians weren't coming to watch Harraden train, and the advance sales for the match were not all that great either.

"Yes indeed," said Gomez, "slow times."

Meanwhile, the first demonstration bout had begun, and Spiegel headed toward the ring.

Harraden was boxing against a large, slightly bloated-looking man with droopy shoulders, thin legs, and an unintelligent expression.

Gomez and Maltravers exchanged glances and shook their heads.

In the second round, Harraden knocked out his sparring partner.

"So much for him."

The sparring partners hired for great prizefighters are generally men who once had prospects of excellent careers, but who, for some reason or other, usually after serious defeats, lost their nerve and could no longer get through a fight. However, since they have to earn a living, they are paid to be beaten up in a demonstration bout. You see, ever since bare fists were made illegal and four-to-six-ounce gloves mandatory, a boxing match has little chance of being settled by a quick knockout, except between heavyweights. Instead, a boxer keeps banging away at his opponent round after round, until the opponent, when standing there openly, can be knocked out by a decisive punch or a series of decisive punches. A gloved fist punching the still unshaken opponent will seldom lead to a decision. However, repeated series of punches can ultimately wear a pugilist down. Sometimes, the resulting shock can trigger a permanent disorder, and boxers who suffer such injuries may, for a while, be first-class opponents, both physically and technically. But within a short time, their morale vanishes. Having become useless for real matches, they try to scrape out a living by waiting for demonstration bouts, in which they act as live sandbags, enduring the worst punches and constantly landing on the ground. They keep getting up, but only to be slugged down again. And if there are no demonstration bouts, they are at a loss as to what to live on, and they go to pot more and more.

Incidentally, such a bout is not necessarily meant only to be a public spectacle advertising the real event or to incite the public to place bets. Rather, these demonstrations help reacclimate the boxers, after a short or long hiatus, to the atmosphere of a ring looming from a huge mob of spectators. They inure the boxers to people's reactions, to the dazzling lights, and to the shouts and shrieks of the audience. For most people go to fights, races, etc., not because they are really interested, but because by yelling or criticizing, they hope to share the limelight at some major event involving a boxer, an actor, a horse, or a gamecock.

Harraden's next opponent was a bony fellow with a low forehead and a mashed nose. He made such a poor showing that he was soon hissed and booed from the ring.

During the ensuing break, Maltravers initially remained silent. Obviously nervous, he kept crossing his right foot over his left and vice versa. Then, all at once, he said: "Would it not be better if we ran along? None of these boys will do. I do not see why I have to go on watching this. I am a failure myself. If you have no better suggestions. . . ."

His voice trailed off, for a new sparring partner had just stepped into the ring.

Maltravers instantly saw that this was a young, unusually handsome man. He later confessed that he had noticed it or rather sensed it before ever setting eyes on him. It was as if something very radiant, with a different light than that of the lamps, had entered the glow of the ring. The new man was tall, actually an inch or two taller than Harraden, and as straight as a lance. Yet a shadow lay on his face, and one could only divine the contour of the dark eyebrows forming a very manly frown and, underneath, the shimmer of the eyes, bluish as if cast by a fire refracted by jewels. His skin gave off something like the brilliance of pure breath.

45

Maltravers glanced at Gomez, and Gomez glanced back, grinning. But Maltravers was already gazing at the ring again. However, the sparring partner seemed to have made no impact on the rest of the audience. Only a single person, a woman in her early forties, suddenly applauded, all alone, frantically, and the other spectators turned to look at her and laughed.

Maltravers was convinced that if he had thought of applauding, they would have laughed at him too. People always laugh at those who notice something unusual. That is their defense whenever they are unsettled. For something unusual is always unsettling; all greatness shakes them, all beauty confuses them. People, however, do not care to be unsettled. They act as if they simply did not see anything uncommon. Maltravers glanced at the woman who had nevertheless applauded, and he told himself that she must have spent an entire lifetime with the most disappointing men in order to applaud like that. Young women do not need to be unusual. It is only when they grow older that some of them become unusual women, and then they are laughed at.

For aging means: belatedly developing an eye for unsettling things, which are life. An eye for danger. Anything unusual is dangerous. Only common things are not dangerous. To really live means to endanger oneself.

Maltravers had courted danger all his life. The only danger he had hated was the one that no one escapes: death. For it accosted everyone, it was utterly common, there was nothing skillful about dying. However, the count began to realize that he must have been mistaken. For one can also pass away in the same manner in which one has lived: personally, even grandiosely, and not just universally like others. And he had been waiting ever since for his second death, somewhat as impatiently as a man who has to even the score.

The gong interrupted his daydreams.

A fight between opponents of different heights ought basically to follow the principle that the man with the longer reach should simply not let the man with the shorter reach get at him. For why be hit if it's not necessary! Harraden's sparring partner, taller and obviously outreaching him, stood utterly straight on the points of his feet, yet leaning slightly forward. Lunging out with straight lefts and occasionally straight rights, and defending himself by means of those same straight punches without ever being hit in return, he slammed a series of hard, resounding punches into his opponent's face. When Harraden, whose nose started bleeding, angrily tried to break through, he was cut off by the gong. However, the instant the second round began, he set about pursuing his goal. Hunched over and evidently also shielded by his padded headguard, he smashed through his opponent's straight punches, landing a left hook on his chin. From that moment on, his sparring partner lost his nerve. He managed to get through the round, but stopped attacking. Ultimately, after enduring several shattering hooks and haymakers, he was saved by the gong. In the third round, however, he promptly double-guarded himself; his body was covered with sweat. He managed to straighten up again, but was then driven to the ropes. He attempted one last attack, but, after getting through a brief, violent exchange of blows, then enduring three or four more hooks without resisting, he went down for the count.

The audience applauded, got up, and went about its business.

When the loser struggled to his feet and was helped

out of the ring, Gomez and Maltravers went over to Harraden's manager. Spiegel was arguing with his fighter, who was now wrapped up in a bathrobe.

"Who was that?" asked Maltravers, tapping Spiegel on the back.

"Who?" asked Spiegel, turning around.

"The other fighter, of course," said Maltravers.

"Him?" asked Spiegel. "He's a sparring partner."

"Yes. But what is his name?"

"Dan Holland. Why?"

"He interests me. I think he fought marvelously, at least at the start."

"Really?" asked Spiegel, taking one of the cigarettes offered by Gomez. "You noticed? Well, he could have made a nice career for himself."

"But?"

"But his luck ran out. He lost his nerve. He was too high-strung. They say his father was a minor official or something not much better in Hanover, I think, or somewhere around there. . . . Koblitz managed him for a while. Then he was kayoed by Ismailski. At first, it looked like an ordinary knockout. But at his next fight, he failed completely. Koblitz saw the handwriting on the wall and simply dumped him. That was two years ago, here in Paris. The kid didn't have a penny to his name. At first, a couple of people tried to help him, but he soon fell in with a bad crowd—people who used him or who kept him more or less. He's been mooching around ever since. Sometimes he's had luck. He was always a good-looking guy. But usually he leads a hand-to-mouth existence. His real name is Henrikstein. But he boxed under the name of Holland, because that's where he grew up."

"Listen," said Maltravers after a pause, "could I speak to him?"

Spiegel eyed him strangely and then said casually: It could be arranged. But he had to talk to Harraden for a while. Eventually, he said he could take the two men to the dressing room.

Gomez and Maltravers stopped outside the door, and Spiegel went in but came back out after a very short time and laughed.

"You're out of luck," he said. "He's taken off."

"What do you mean?" asked Maltravers. "Why?"

"When I told him two gentlemen wanted to see him, he probably thought he was gonna be nabbed. He just took off. He must've done something."

Now Gomez laughed, and took down Henrikstein's address. Then he left with the count.

FOUR

As it turned out, Henrikstein lived in a tiny, sordid rooming house, but when Gomez and Maltravers arrived, he had not yet come home. The two men said they would wait. Well, they'd have to wait a good long time, said the woman who took them to Henrikstein's room. "Edgar" often didn't come home till very late at night, and he'd be off again in the morning. Sometimes, he'd stay out all night. He was also behind with the rent.

The woman looked disheveled and nervous, and Maltravers thought to himself that Henrikstein must have his reasons for avoiding her, even if he did not owe her all that much back rent.

Settling down on two chairs with damaged straw plaiting, the visitors lit cigarettes. At first, they kept silent as they looked around the shabbily furnished room; a few of Henrikstein's toilet articles and a pile of old newspapers lay there, and a threadbare suit hung in a half-open closet. Henrikstein's passport lay on the night table. They examined it. It was a German passport, made out to Edgar Daniel Henrikstein, also known as Holland, born in Celle, twenty-three years old. Eventually Gomez said: "We won't find a more suitable person. That family in Hanover needn't have been the worst, and we can hope that he's picked up some manners and not forgotten them entirely. On the other hand, his troubles can't have hurt him all too much. Otherwise, he wouldn't look as good as he does. . . . In any case, his predicament must be bad enough for him to go along unprotestingly with anything we suggest."

"I have no intention," said Maltravers, "of telling him the truth."

"Why not?"

"It would prevent him from being spontaneous."

"But how is he supposed to know what to do?"

"It will come out of the situation. He will be easily influenced, like all people with defects."

"Whatever you say," said Gomez. "Incidentally, I spoke to Levasseur again today. He's getting a bit edgy. However, I told him that this sort of thing can't be rushed. But now we've got what we're looking for. How long do you think we'll need to get the boy ready?"

"A couple of days. By the way, what does the woman look like?"

"Mme. Levasseur? She looks pretty good."

"Really?"

"Yes."

"Young?"

"She looks twenty-six or twenty-seven. But she's thirty."

"I'd prefer thirty-five."

"Why?"

"Because that is when women first start realizing what they have missed. Earlier than that, they miss, but they do not realize it. Today, when the boy was in the ring, only one woman applauded. But she was past forty. At that age, a woman needs no great skill to see that a young man is handsome. . . . Otherwise, however, women are far too practical to indulge in noticing beauty. It is simply too dangerous for them. They already know in regard to themselves how dangerous beauty can be. Except that at times they simply cannot help themselves. . . . Well, once the boy is decently dressed. . . . We shall see. . . ."

They waited until eleven P.M., but Henrikstein did not come. Finally, they wrote a few words on a slip of paper, more or less to the effect that they only wished to see him on business and that they would come back the next morning. They left the note on the table. When they came back the next day, the note was gone, and so was Henrikstein, even though he had been home at some point. He had not had the nerve to remain, nor did he appear the next day or the day after. He had not called either, for the rooming house had no telephone, which, incidentally, would have been superfluous, for the Paris telephone system was not functioning anyway. Gomez was growing nervous. Finally, Maltravers stationed himself alone at the building entrance, telling himself that this was the only way to get hold of Henrikstein, for the boxer knew neither Gomez nor Maltravers. But Henrikstein did not show up. However, another young man did, and he put Maltravers on Henrikstein's track.

You see, this young man, who appeared toward four in the afternoon, aroused the count's suspicions by lingering outside the building and in the doorway, and peering around for an extremely long time before entering. He was also leading a large, white poodle, which, being apparently very valuable, did not fit in with the young man's shabbiness. Furthermore, the dog had obviously just been shorn, and in such a peculiar and unwonted fashion that Maltravers instantly sensed that the dog had been kidnapped and completely recoiffured.

When the young man with the poodle had vanished inside the house, Maltravers hurried after him and saw that he was indeed buzzing Henrikstein's bell. Maltravers instantly returned to the street. A short time later, the young man likewise came out again, taking off with his dog. Maltravers followed him. The young man walked several blocks, finally stepping into a small café. Maltravers was just about to enter it when the young man reappeared out with Henrikstein.

Upon seeing the boxer, Maltravers breathed a sigh of relief. He wanted to go right up to him and explain that he absolutely had to speak to him. But he did not have a chance. For Henrikstein walked or, rather, ran off, constantly arguing with the other man as they headed down the street, dragging along the dog. Obviously, they were arguing mainly about the dog, for Henrikstein kept pointing at it agitatedly. Meanwhile, they dashed along, and the count had a difficult time keeping up. All at once, Henrikstein stopped at a building entrance, and the other man vanished inside with the dog.

Maltravers walked straight up to Henrikstein, who had turned and was looking around. For the first time, the count saw Henrikstein's face up close. It was very youthful and clear, perhaps just a tad too broad near the cheekbones. But the complexion was conspicuously pure, the nose straight, and the eyes were large and gray, with a vaguely bluish shimmer. When the count approached, the eyes widened even further, darkening, while the pupils grew larger, as if fearing the stranger. Realizing that if he addressed Henrikstein, the boxer would instantly run off again, the count made a quick last-minute decision and walked past him as if intending to go on.

But some twenty paces later, he halted; he could avoid being conspicuous since the street was fairly animated. Glancing back, he saw that Henrikstein, who had obviously calmed down, was still standing in the same place. Now Maltravers remained standing too, wondering how he could finally address Henrikstein. But meanwhile, the other young man reemerged from the house, this time without the poodle, and the two men headed back in the direction from which they had come. Well, the mountain is certainly not coming to Mohammed, the count thought to himself, and he had no choice but to follow them again.

About two minutes later, they boarded an omnibus, and Maltravers likewise got in. He was afraid he would now draw Henrikstein's attention, but Henrikstein did not notice him in the throng. Inside the bus, the two young men no longer conversed. They merely stood there, shaken by the movements of the vehicle. They got out at Gare du Nord, as did Maltravers, and they strode into the railroad station, halting and lighting cigarettes. They smoked and peered around. They were obviously observing the people coming from the arriving trains. The terminal was already illuminated, although it was still daylight outside. Suddenly, the two young men tossed away their cigarettes and went out into the street again.

At first, Maltravers did not understand what it was all about, but he quickly saw that the two of them were concentrating on a man who had probably just arrived. He was of medium height, bony, and spirited, obviously from the country, probably northern France. His only luggage was a small satchel. The young men followed him when he left the station. He went over to the bus stop and read the signs. But he let several buses pass, and he never got into one. He had probably, thought Maltravers, not visited Paris very often and was disoriented about the buses. In any case, he finally headed toward the center of the city on foot.

The instant the two young men saw which direction he was taking, Henrikstein began to precede him by some three paces, and Henrikstein's friend preceded Henrikstein by ten paces. Maltravers sensed what would happen next. Indeed, all at once, Henrikstein bent over as if picking something up, and the bumpkin, who was not paying attention, ran into him. But since Henrikstein was still bent over, the man also bent over. Both of them then straightened up, Henrikstein was holding something he had picked up and was looking at it, and the man from the country looked at it too. They were looking at a glittering object, evidently a piece of jewelry or a ring. Next, Maltravers suspected, Henrikstein's friend would come back and join them, and indeed his friend turned around at that moment and joined the other two.

Maltravers likewise paused at a certain distance. He could not hear what the three men were talking about, but he easily guessed. The whole thing was an extremely simple kind of flimflam, often practiced and often described, but still as effective as ever.

Henrikstein's friend had dropped an obviously worthless ring, and the boxer had picked it up in such a way that the hayseed would have to notice it and believe that Henrikstein had found a truly valuable ring, not paste; for in his rustic imagination, the streets of Paris were paved with real jewels. There was no question of imitations.

Henrikstein also grimaced as if he were embarrassed

that someone had noticed him picking up the ring, and this convinced the rustic all the more that the find was very precious. Now it is often very difficult for two people to establish some kind of contact or rapport. But they easily manage, if they suddenly find themselves doing something illicit together, or if one wishes to prevent the other from doing it because he wants to do it himself or at least participate.

Henrikstein would not wish to turn the ring over to anyone—the rustic took that for granted, but he was also determined not to let him have the ring all for himself; he would demand some share or at least hush money. Furthermore, any last doubts he might have had about the value of the ring were dispelled when Henrikstein's friend came over.

For his friend spotted the ring and asked: What did they have there? A ring? They had found it? It looked authentic, beyond doubt. Very valuable! Naturally, it had to be turned in to the police!

His interference created an embarrassed silence. Then Henrikstein and the rustic exchanged glances, indicating that they would work together, and Henrikstein said: Yes, the ring would be turned in, but he, Henrikstein, had found it; he alone would turn it in and obtain the reward; it was no one else's concern. Well, cried Henrikstein's friend, but he was a witness and he would make sure there was no monkey business. . . . Was he casting suspicion on him! cried Henrikstein. In short, after the discussion had dragged on for a while and the sucker was sufficiently convinced of the value of the ring, Henrikstein's friend took off after swallowing a few gross insults from the boxer. He seemed deeply offended, but slipped around the next corner, waiting for the outcome of the financial debate that followed.

For when Henrikstein was once again alone with the

simpleton, he suddenly told him that the whole matter was starting to worry him; he was willing to share the take, only the other man would have to offer it to a dealer; it was too dangerous for Henrikstein. Now the simpleton began to feel queasy. But Henrikstein went on: He wanted to wash his hands of the matter, and he was willing to give the man the ring in exchange for a certain amount of money.

The rustic had become so greedy that he took the bait and started haggling about the indemnity. The dickering dragged on for a while. Finally, they seemed to have come to terms, and the simpleton was about to hand over some banknotes, which would have settled the matter as planned—if something unexpected had not occurred.

Henrikstein and the rustic had been haggling so intensely, and Maltravers had been watching so closely, that no one spotted two policemen who were observing the scene. The police usually keep an eye out for suspicious doings around the terminal, and just as Henrikstein was about to take hold of the other man's money, the uniformed arm of the law reached for his shoulder.

Maltravers felt a pang when he saw that they were about to take Henrikstein away from him and lock him up, probably for several months. The count wanted to do something, warn him, but it was too late. However, he had not reckoned with Henrikstein's outstanding physical qualities. Henrikstein instantly skedaddled in an exemplary way. He zoomed off with the speed and agility of an athlete, which he was, after all.

However, the officers, who apparently considered him more important than the simpleton, stormed after him no less speedily, and the pursuers and their quarry disappeared around the next corner.

Maltravers heaved a sigh of relief. On the other

hand, he told himself that Henrikstein had escaped him again. Muttering a curse, he threw down the cigarette that he had just lit, stepped on it, and walked off roughly in the direction in which the runners had vanished. The count had been hunting Henrikstein for days now and he foresaw that it would take days to find him if ever he did lay eyes on him again, which was questionable. Maltravers halted, lighting another cigarette. At that instant, he was almost knocked to the ground by a man who came dashing around a corner. It was Henrikstein, who had doubled back, scurried around the block, and was now racing along.

Maltravers instantly saw that he had to seize this perhaps last chance of getting hold of Henrikstein, even if it meant risking his own freedom. The boxer had likewise staggered back from the collision. Maltravers grabbed his arm and whispered to him in German;

"Come on! I'll tell them we were strolling here together!"

Henrikstein did not seem to catch Maltravers's drift. He did not know him, nor did he understand why a perfect stranger should come to his aid. But since the words were, first of all, in German, and, second of all, whispered (two circumstances of which the second, at that time, was as German as the first, and which, altogether, inspired the listener to have confidence in something illicit), Henrikstein, after a final, involuntary movement, as if he did wish to run off after all, halted next to Maltravers, panting and gasping.

"Stop gasping!" the count hissed. "They'll be here any second!" And linking arms with Henrikstein, he led him back in the direction from which he had come dashing.

A moment later, they stood in front of the pursuing

officers. That is, when the two men came toward them, the policemen at first did not consider them suspicious. They ran by, then thought it over since they saw no one running ahead of them. Turning on their heels, they tried to grab Henrikstein.

The count intently clutched Henrikstein's sleeve, gaped at the policemen, and asked: "What is it you wish, gentlemen?"

"That's him!" shouted the officers and seized Henrikstein.

"Who?" asked Maltravers.

The man who had run away from them, they managed to gasp out, struggling for air.

Who had run away? asked the count.

"This guy here!" shouted the policemen.

Why, they must be mistaken, cried the count. He had been strolling with this young man for a long time now, and he had certainly not been running. What was this all about anyway! He would show them his papers, he was Count Fortescue—and he pulled out his passport —the young man was Edgar Henrikstein, and the officers must have been chasing someone else, not this young man, and so forth.

Meanwhile, a crowd was gathering, and the policemen, now unsure of themselves, asked whether some other young man had come running by.

"Possibly," said Maltravers. "In any case we have not been running, so if you gentlemen could please detain us no further, all this attention is not very pleasant!" And taking Henrikstein by the arm again, he pushed through the crowd, and the police pushed through the crowd in their direction and hurried off, hoping to catch their prey.

As he and Henrikstein moved off, Maltravers, shaking his head, addressed the throng, which was still gawking at them. He said he simply did not understand what the police wanted. But no sooner was he alone with Henrikstein than he told him that they would have to get away from here. He hailed a cab, gave the driver the address of a café, pushed Henrikstein into the cab, and got in himself.

"I have been looking for you for days," he said as the cab started off. "I even dropped by your room and left you a note. But you have been gadding about, cheating people, exposing yourself to possible arrest. And just what was that flashy poodle your friend had?"

"Oh," exclaimed Henrikstein, "I told him it was crazy trying to sell it! He had cut it loose, but when I tried to bring it back to get a reward, the police had already come, and we had to keep the poodle. But why are you interested in all this? Where do you know me from anyway? Who are you?"

The count answered him tersely. Meanwhile, the cab was already pulling up in front of the café. "In any case," murmured Henrikstein as they stepped out, "I'm very grateful to you for saving me from that situation. . . . "

"But why," asked Henrikstein "did you do it? What did you want to talk to me about?"

"I will explain everything," said Maltravers.

And they entered the café.

FIVE

Several days later, when Maltravers visited the agent again, Gomez happened to be at the window, gazing at the street, which was rather noisy, so that he did not hear the count enter, and when Gomez turned around, Maltravers was already standing in the middle of the room.

Gomez jumped. Then he rubbed his brow and shook his head.

"My goodness," he said, "you've recently developed a nice way of startling people! Honestly, if you hadn't kept assuring me that you've come back to life, I would've sworn you were still dead."

Maltravers laughed.

"Would you," he asked, "find that so disagreeable? After all, Gomez, you yourself are shortly going to find yourself in that state."

"I know!" cried the broker. "But I don't care to be reminded of it all the time. Please, just tell me the news."

"Well," said Maltravers, settling on the edge of the

desk and poking his cane into Gomez's papers, "the news is that we are dining with the Levasseurs at the Grand Veneur."

"Fancy that! And what about the boy? How is he handling it?"

"Quite well."

"And how does he find the woman?"

"Whom?"

"Madame Levasseur!"

"He has not met her as yet."

"How come? What have you been doing with him all this time?"

"This and that."

"Namely?"

"First of all, I had to order a couple of suits for him. That was rather difficult. For the French tailors work very badly, while the foreigners here work far too well. The boy is so attractive that he would look downright repulsive in a well-made suit. So I had them turn out a few suits that do not fit him so well, which caused me endless trouble with the tailors. But I finally found a little Bohemian tailor who did what I wanted. Do not shake your head, Gomez; you know nothing about such matters. Your wardrobe is exemplarily awful. By the way, I had a lot of problems with the linen, shoes, and hats for the boy. For everything showed him to his best advantage. I had to keep selecting things that showed him at a disadvantage. In general, nonadvantageous things are more advantageous than advantageous things. The day before yesterday—"

"I don't understand."

"It does not matter," said Maltravers. "Anyhow, the day before yesterday, he got himself a manicure, obviously in order to please me—for he is a good boy. I had to reprimand him severely. A gentleman, I said, is not

64

manicured. A gentleman has to be neglectful of his person. I told him that he looks so good as he is that he must neglect himself continuously in order not to draw attention. I have also been supervising his manners. Although there is nothing effeminate about him, he adapts as easily as a woman or other creatures blessed by nature. His background is very humble, but within just a few days of observing me, he acquired such fine manners that it became unbearable. A gentleman, I said, is not supposed to have manners. One simply should not notice that he has manners. And so forth and so forth. Dressing an attractive woman is a pleasure, but when everything fits a young man so easily, it is downright embarrassing. One always suspects goodness knows what. I am at a loss to understand why no one else has thought of capitalizing on his looks. But evidently no one has an eye for such things. People always notice only the packaging. Without packaging, they see nothing. Otherwise, it would not have been possible for someone like Otero to roam about in a Gypsy wagon for years on end until she was finally discovered. And do you know who discovered her?"

"No."

"I did," said Maltravers.

"You?"

"Yes. But that was a long time ago, and all I was driving at, dear Gomez, is that the eye is everything. The world does not exist, it must be created over and over again. It is created by the eye. I have never worked a day in my life; I have simply always had an eye for other people. But I fancy I have achieved more in that way than if I had worked all the time."

"Indeed," said the agent. "You've accomplished amazing things. No doubt about it!"

"One also has to be able to squander, my good

Gomez. When one dies, one ought to have squandered everything one has achieved."

"Except," said the agent, "that for you the equation did not work out."

"But for you," said Maltravers, peering around the office, "it will, I fear, work out. Apropos squandering," he went on, while the agent vehemently shook his head, "we have been living in the Claridge since yesterday—a both expensive and unpleasant hotel. I hate it. It is the sort of place at which my sister-in-law would be certain to stay if she came to Paris."

"What sister-in-law?"

"My brother's wife. Let us not talk about her. I, in any case, could just as readily have remained at the Saint-Jean, but you asked me to move out. . . . ."

"Of course! We could not have told Madame Levasseur that you live in such a shabby hotel! I find the Claridge very nice."

"Listen, Gomez, what did your father do?"

"Why?"

"You have a taste for the pompous."

"He did nothing pompous."

"Precisely, precisely. What *did* he do?"

"First he was a mule driver, and later on he owned a fruit store."

"What about your mother?"

"My mother worked in a cigarette factory."

Maltravers kept silent for a moment, then said: "The boy's father was a clerk in Celle, near Hanover. His grandfather was supposedly a driver, that is, a coachman or something of that ilk. His mother was a small seamstress. He does not know what his maternal grandfather did. His grandmothers must have been market women. The seamstress died of carcinoma while still young; the boy was only three. When his

66

father died later on—of consumption, I think—the child was taken in by a relative in Holland, a butcher. Well, a coachman's grandchild and butcher's ward can eventually turn into a boxer. But please explain to me how the son of a clerk and a seamstress can look like an aristocrat—if, of course, aristocrats look as we picture them!"

"That," said Gomez, "is typical aristocratic astonishment. He looks as he looks, simply because commoners very often look a lot better than aristocrats."

"But you, dear Gomez, still look as if you drove mules in your leisure hours."

"And you look like a prince, which did not prevent you from cheating at cards."

"On the contrary, that was what enabled me to cheat in the first place."

"Well, there you are!"

"I once knew a Baron Himmelberg," said Maltravers, "who studied various sciences and who claimed, among other things, that human beings once lived from hunting, especially from hunting reindeer and wild horses. In France alone, he said, the factories still purchased thousands of tons of bones from these prehistoric wild horses for some kind of industrial processing. For so many wild horses once existed, he said, that the bones of the captured animals could still be found everywhere. But when the glaciers retreated, the wildlife migrated northward. Some human beings switched over to farming; the others, however, followed the animals. This Himmelberg claimed that the descendants of the tillers of the soil are the ordinary nations, while the descendants of the hunters, who remained 'in the wild' are the noble nations."

"What difference does he see between them? And besides, is that all you have to report?"

"No," laughed Maltravers. "But what do you wish to know?"

"For instance: How does he feel about tonight?"

"Who?"

"The boy, of course."

"Well, I told him we would be going out with friends, and he said he would love it!"

"That's all?"

"No."

"I mean: Is that all you said to him?"

"No. I have already told you: I do not plan to tell him anything. After all, you claim that the woman is attractive."

"What if he is *not* attracted to her?"

"That is quite possible, to be sure. For I believe he is attracted to someone else."

"What do you mean? Who?"

"A certain Mademoiselle Lola Nowy, but she calls herself Lolita."

"Who the devil is *she*?"

"A dancer in a nightclub where we went the first evening. To begin with, we drove from Gare du Nord to a café. I told him I had seen him box against Harraden, and I had very much enjoyed his style. I said I was sure that a great future lay ahead of him. He looked askance at me and said I probably thought so only because I knew nothing about boxing. Oh but I did, I said. I knew a great deal about it, and that was why I simply could not believe that his career was really over. His defects, I said, were only nervous ones, and so they could be cured by his morale. He only had to regain the self-confidence he had lost. This was, of course, not possible, given his present milieu and the life he was leading. He simply had to get a new lease on life. How? he laughed. In prison maybe? He saw no other possibility of changing himself. Then I should have let the police grab him. In short, I saw he was not deceiving himself in any way; his eyes were fully open to his condition. But I said it made no sense to concentrate only on training. Indeed, for the time being, he ought to drop his training altogether. He would actually have to forget that he had ever been in the ring, and he would have to start an entirely different life. I told him that, I was in a position to offer him this chance. He looked at me and said that I should come right out and tell him exactly what I wanted from him. Just what I had already told him, I replied: I still considered him a contender. He could view it as a whim, for all I cared, but I truly had every intention of investing money in his future. I was interested in seeing whether a broken-down boxer could make a comeback. He was to live according to my instructions for a while, have a good time, restore his nerves, and only then would he reenter the ring. I do not know whether or not he truly believed me. But he acted as if he did. After all, he had nothing to lose; at most, a lot to gain. Nevertheless, a silence ensued. Evidently, he was thinking about my true intentions. It is obvious that he did not guess them. But I was starting to believe my own words. Why, ultimately, should I not be able to help this man get back on his feet, aside from having him serve our needs? It would be criminal to leave such a beautiful and also unhappy creature to his fate if he might possibly be saved. After all, he does not have to make a comeback. He can pursue a career in the circles into which I plan to introduce him. Before and during the meal that I ordered, I spoke to him for hours on end—"

"But why?" Gomez broke in. "You were probably just dangling completely false hopes before him, which can never come true. Yet you did not so much as hint at what you really want him to do, and it is questionable whether he will do it. You yourself find it questionable. You should simply have told him straight out—"

"Gomez," said Maltravers, "you can be sure that I will never tell him. It suffices completely if I alone assume the responsibility for what will actually happen. It would be quite superfluous to burden this boy, who is defective anyway. He must believe that he is acting correctly. That way, he will be far more successful. I have already told you that I regard correctness as far more successful than incorrectness."

"Honestly," said Gomez, "for a man who has gone through such irregularities as you have lately, your views are quite moralistic!"

"Naturally," said Maltravers, "otherwise I would not have them. And believe me, Gomez, immorality is not in our nature. It is really a great pleasure to be moral. One always has to force oneself to be immoral. When all is said and done, God permits immorality in the world to keep morality sensational, since—as I must confess—like all pleasures, it could ultimately become boring. Being immoral is worse. For a while, I was immoral enough to be able to appreciate morality again. Allow me my fun, Gomez!"

"Tell me," asked the agent, "do you actually believe what you're saying? Do you even understand it?"

"Yes," said Maltravers. "That is, no . . . or perhaps, not entirely."

"Then perhaps you might tell me what happened with that woman! I mean the nightclub dancer."

"Well," said Maltravers, "we got there around eleven in the evening. When talking to the boy, I had tried above all to imbue him with self-confidence. For I realized he had none. As we know, he has always been a failure. Failing means having more confidence in others than in oneself. During the two years he has been living in Paris, he has, no doubt, been constantly exploited and misused by others, and he has probably endured an incredible number of disappointments. He could not recall a single instance of desiring something and attaining it. For example, despite his good looks, he no longer managed to impress the women he liked, plainly because such women noticed that he was a has-been, and if they did not reach out to him themselves, they would simply send him packing. At the Chapeau Rouge—"

"That's where you were?"

"Yes. Anyway, at the Chapeau Rouge, after the final performance, the chorines came over to the tables and chatted with the customers, or else they waited around at the bar, and I noticed one girl. She was not the prettiest, but for some reason she made a good impression on me, above all because she was a natural blonde and her hair was not just idiotically dyed. She was standing at a distance from us, talking to another dancer."

"'Do you see that young woman?' I said to Henrikstein. 'If you go over and talk to her, she is certain to like you, not because it is her duty to be friendly to the customers or because she would be fired if she so much as dreamt of getting impudent, but because she will really like you.'

"He looked at me, unsure of himself, but stood up and walked over to her. They began to chat, and I noticed that she was not smiling at him with the stupid expression that girls in these places usually have when they talk to men. Even though he was young and shabbily dressed—two things that make a man completely uninteresting to such a girl—she nevertheless seemed a wee bit interested. After a while, he came back and asked me if he could invite her to join us.

71

"Her name, as I have said, is Lola or Lolita, and she soon turned out to be a truly charming person. She was of average height, very young, still a bit tender, and not conspicuously pretty, but she had an utterly appealing way of speaking and moving. When one talks to girls in such clubs, they have the dreadful habit of constantly executing dancelike steps, warbling, restlessly swinging their arms—in short, behaving like creatures that automatically keep doing whatever has been drilled into them. Lola, however, stood there in a decent posture until she sat down with us. Nor was she spruced up like a typical dancer, who besmears her empty face with an even emptier one. Instead, she had kept her natural expression, her eyebrows curved by themselves, as they should, and she had a sensible gaze, a clear complexion, and lovely hands. In order to make her feel good, I expressed my amazement at finding her in these surroundings. She replied that she had, in fact, only been here a short time. Her French was very poor. I asked her where she came from. She told me to guess. I addressed her in English although I could tell that she was not British. Then I addressed her in Hungarian, Bohemian, and finally I tried a few words in Russian and Italian. She replied in Italian, asking me why I knew so many languages. I said I could also have addressed her in German and Rumanian. She said she could have responded even better in German than Italian. She comes from Fiume, and subsequently we learned that her father had had a position in the merchant marine, after previously serving as a torpedo junior officer or something of the sort.

"She appeared to like Henrikstein very much, and I had the impression that he too was very happy about her interest. We chatted with her very pleasantly for about two hours, and I entirely forgot that I had been

72

in prison, that Henrikstein was a has-been, and that she was actually a B-girl. When we left, she asked us to come again. She said she usually had to converse with such unpleasant men. Indeed, the next day, the boy asked me quite on his own whether we might go back to the Chapeau Rouge. And ever since, we have been there every evening."

"Why, that's," cried Gomez, "that's senseless matchmaking."

"What do you expect!" laughed Maltravers. "I am an old man. All old people like to matchmake."

"Oh, but isn't three a crowd?"

"I do not think so. Remembering my own youth, I am accustomed to a very different determination among young people who like each other, and I was quite astonished that these two young people—whose love I delight in watching, of course—seem to have no intention of getting rid of me. They are content to chat with one another. What do you think of that? They must be truly in love."

"Oh," shouted the agent. "You're really an old jackass, damn it. What have you done? I thought you were going to get the boy interested in Madame Levasseur! Instead, you're indulging in a sort of family life with him and a girl whom, in earlier days, you wouldn't even have hired as a kitchenmaid for your wife!"

"Which wife?" asked Maltravers. "I had two, and each had the charm of a thousand women. . . . No, dear Gomez, the fact is that I am probably somehow touched by the mentality of today's young people. It is a lot cleaner than ours was. . . . Incidentally, do not get nervous. If the girl becomes inconvenient, I will simply send her away. Henrikstein, I believe, cares for her mainly because he has begun a more humane life with this acquaintanceship. That can explain a certain affec-

73

tion for her. But if I want to, I can talk him out of any attachment. He is very easily swayed, and he is not the first person I have swayed. . . . Incidentally, why must he be interested in Madame Levasseur? It will suffice if she is interested in him. After all, it is better to do a woman a favor than to have her do you a favor."

"And you believe. . . ."

"A gentleman," said Maltravers, "is always accommodating."

Gomez fell silent. Eventually, he shrugged, saying: "Whatever you think. Any failure would work mainly against you." And opening a drawer, he handed the count a slip of paper. "Here," he said. "Take it, all the same."

"What is it?" asked Maltravers.

"A check."

"At the moment, I do not need anything."

"C'mon! Take it!"

"All right," said Maltravers, pocketing the check without looking at it. "But basically, I am no longer interested in the financial side of the matter. I am interested in the matter per se. When I died, death felt like something infinitely calming. However, there is something very attractive about starting all over again. I myself, to be sure, am too old for that. But a young man who lives in my stead, who begins where I ended, who, under my guidance, does what I would do if I were young again after my entire life, a young Maltravers, like myself so many, many years ago . . . his successes would have to be incredible! And I, I would be happy to see him ascend without having to torment myself with all the things that help one ascend: traveling, relationships, women, and all those ludicrous details. For example, is it not a much greater pleasure, instead of having to turn women's heads, merely to admire the man who turns their heads? Every life, they say, is a novel. How lovely novels are if one does not have to write them oneself, and how wonderful a life is if one does not live it oneself.

SIX

The Grand Veneur was a relatively new restaurant, unfamiliar to the count, though not one of those faddish places frequented for a few months by people who have money or claim to have had some and who now run up charge accounts with the waiters—ultimately forgetting everything, the place, the waiters, and the charge accounts, as they visit newly opened restaurants. At the Grand Veneur, confidence men without money were thrown out if their bills were not paid by confidence men with money. For only the latter will pay for the former. Furthermore, the restaurant was so expensive that, thereby spreading a kind of terror, it was bound to survive for years. The decorations vividly reminded the count of the wing he had occupied in Sobotitz; for the walls were covered with hunting scenes, antlers, buffalo heads, and the like, as if the people who came to dine here were to be reminded of their homes, where they had never fed on anything but venison. There were also pictures of uniforms, miniatures, and candelabras filled with wax candles everywhere, to make the patrons believe they were still in some castle. And no one dared to admit that he had previously lived otherwise.

The Levasseurs had not yet arrived. Maltravers and Henrikstein were led into a small, but pompously appointed *chambre séparée*, where a table was set for four. Here too the walls were covered with Ridinger engravings and antlers, and at the bottom of the paneling, which ran all around the room, a huge mass of small, thick books were crowded together: military registers, Gothas, and aristocratic pocketbooks from every corner of the world, as Maltravers could tell at a glance.

Henrikstein and the count were immediately served cocktails; they lit cigarettes, and some muted music, played evidently by Gypsies, could be heard from the next room. Maltravers took a flower from the table and inserted it in the lapel of Henrikstein's tuxedo. Then he said:

"My dear Edgar, I am convinced that we shall dine well here, probably even very well. But actually this is not the sort of place one should frequent. It is too tasteful. One should patronize only slightly tasteless restaurants, where one is never disturbed by any kind of style. At bottom, there is something inauthentic about style. People have style only if they have nothing else. Truly good people have no style, anymore than they are exclusive. For they do not compromise themselves no matter whom they associate with. Only people who are nothing cannot afford to associate with just anyone. Nor do I see why I should spend hours here staring at the antlers of sixteen-pointers, which other people, who have never hunted, claim they like. It is unforgivable to force one's own untruths on other people; it is almost as bad as forcing truths upon them. Perhaps the Levasseurs really did not give it a second thought when they invited us here. Or perhaps they do like the place. Well, we shall see. In any case, I will tell them that you are my secretary. I could also simply say I met you while traveling. But I would rather the Levasseurs had a slightly uncomfortable feeling that they are faced with an unclear situation. Nothing is more amusing than letting people guess what they should suspect one of. They are always annoyed that they do not have the courage to do such things themselves. For they would certainly feel like doing anything. . . ."

Henrikstein laughed. "Count," he said, "you can tell the Levasseurs whatever you like. But they should notice that I admire you. . . ."

"Ah," murmured Maltravers, "you should not. One is close only to the people whom one does not respect. With others, one does not feel one is among peers. . . ."

At that point, the Levasseurs came in.

"Count Fortescue," said Levasseur, "I must beg you to forgive our tardiness. But I believe that my wife was truly delighted when I told her what charming people she would be meeting. For it took her forever to dress. Whenever my wife takes her time, it is a sign of her interest. She is punctual only when she is utterly uninterested. Lisette, may I present Count Fortescue and Monsieur Henrikstein."

Levasseur, still one of the leading heavy industrialists of France, was relatively young, forty-four or -five, of medium height, with dark, but thinning hair. In private, his manner may have been slightly too decisive. Lisette Levasseur thanked the count for the roses he had sent her, then she offered Henrikstein her hand. Her eyes suddenly widened, and she had difficulty concealing the impression the young man made on her. Maltravers saw it and glanced in the air for a moment.

Madame Levasseur was tall and slender, perhaps a smidgen taller than her husband. She was exceedingly attractive, her hair was shiny black, and she wore few, but utterly beautiful jewels. Her clothing stood out. Yet there was a trace of uncertainty in her movements, such as one sees in women from a milieu humbler than the one in which they have to move. It was noticeable the instant she met Henrikstein. He said something, but she did not immediately know how to respond and she lowered her eyes. Another round of cocktails was served, and Madame Levasseur was also doing something with her coat and her bag. It may have been a leftover from childhood, but she seemed to have a habit of not quite knowing what to do with her hands. The foursome exchanged a few indifferent words while standing, then they seated themselves for dinner.

No one mentioned how Levasseur had met the count. At first, Maltravers chatted with Mme. Levasseur, then he left it up to Henrikstein to entertain her. Henrikstein acted very spontaneously, and Maltravers nodded very faintly at him, smiling. Levasseur spoke to the count about the weather and French politics. Mme. Levasseur said very little. Now and then, she virtually performed some very minor duty as the hostess. Otherwise she listened to Henrikstein, raising her eyes only moments at a time, and Maltravers wondered whether this was her usual demeanor.

They were served by three waiters, one of whom supervised. He was a somewhat pudgy man with great assurance when giving instructions and when occasionally participating in the service. He spoke with the so-called *accent de l'est*, a pronunciation typical of Burgundy and Lorraine. When he lit a cigar for Maltravers after the meal, he bent down to him, asking something in an undertone that the count did not immediately understand. It was only a moment later that he realized it had been in Russian, and that the waiter had asked whether he should bring Russian liquor.

"By all means," replied Maltravers in French. "Are you Russian?"

"No, Your Lordship."

"How do you know Russian?"

"I learned it in Russia, where Your Lordship also learned it. At least, Your Lordship spoke it very fluently when you and Herr von Rosenthorpe brought the czar those chickens, which, given the prevailing circumstances, the czar most likely did not enjoy as much as Monsieur le Comte, hopefully, enjoyed the poulardes tonight."

Maltravers frowned, replying only after a few seconds. "I believe you are confusing me with someone else."

"I do not think so," said the waiter. "Monsieur le Comte did understand my Russian very well."

"For whom do you take me?"

"Count Maltravers."

Maltravers glanced at the others. Only Levasseur was listening. His wife was conversing with Henrikstein at the other end of the table.

"I have already told you," the count turned back to the waiter, "that you are confusing me with someone else. My name is not Maltravers. It is Fortescue."

"Yes," said the waiter, "Fortescue-Maltravers." Levasseur's eyes kept darting between the count and the waiter; he seemed to be wondering what this was all about. Maltravers stared at the waiter, but could obviously not recall having ever laid eyes on him before.

"Your Lordship does not remember me," said the waiter. "But I remember Monsieur le Comte very well. It must—" and he began to count on his fingers—"It must have been three or perhaps even four days prior to that eighteenth of July. . . . I can no longer remember the name of the small station, to be sure, but it was in the area of Ufa, where Monsieur le Comte and Herr von Rosenthorpe joined our so-called court procession. Of course, the gentlemen were wearing peasant garb and had long beards. Herr von Rosenthorpe had two chickens in a basket. But Monsieur le Comte was grasping two loudly clucking chickens, whose legs were tied. . . ."

"Listen," Maltravers snapped, "what are you talking about? Just who are you?"

"My name," said the waiter, "is Antoine Mercoeur. I come from Nancy, and I had the honor of being the czar's last groom of the chamber."

"What?" said Levasseur, astonished. "What were you?"

In France, there are still a huge number of Russian emigrés who claim to have been any number of things, but their stories are seldom believed. However, since Maltravers seemed oddly moved, Levasseur peered at the waiter and the count, but without managing to glean from the latter's face whether or not he actually recognized this Mercoeur.

"It is a mistake!" the count said finally. "I am not the man he thinks I am."

"Who does he think you are?"

"How should *I* know? After all, I do not know who he is."

"Or," asked the waiter, "does Monsieur le Comte find it unpleasant that I should remember that whole business?"

"I cannot," said Maltravers, "forbid you from re-membering something that I know or something that I do not know. By all means, remember anything you care to remember. But I, in any case, remember nothing. Where would one be if one remembered everything?"

"Or perhaps," said the waiter, "Monsieur le Comte does not wish to speak about those things because Monsieur le Comte has claimed through the newspapers that he is dead?"

Levasseur must have found this remark utterly in-comprehensible. But since Maltravers held his tongue, Levasseur finally asked:

"Who is dead? And," he turned to the waiter, "were you really the groom of the czar's chamber?"

"I had the honor," said Mercoeur, "to hold that position."

"How did you get here?"

"I returned to France," said Mercoeur, "shortly after the imperial family were shot."

"And what about Monsieur le Comte," asked Levas-seur, "do you really think. . . . " But he broke off, gaz-ing at Maltravers.

However, the count said, "Keep asking. He claims he saw me somewhere. I have no idea what occasion he is alluding to. But this business is starting to interest me too. Nothing is more interesting than being mistaken for someone else. It expands the horizon of one's exis-tence, as it were. For one has the pleasant sensation that one may be leading other lives as well, lives one knows nothing about. . . . "

"Monsieur le Comte," said Mercoeur, "is probably in-dicating that Monsieur le Comte would finally like to know how the whole business ended after you jumped from the train. For Monsieur le Comte still does not know for sure after all these years. Almost no one knows, and there were no reports on it. But I know."

"Then," said Maltravers casually, leaning back in his armchair, "stop beating about the bush! But first, please tell us what you are driving at. For we really do not know what you are talking about. First of all, who or what are you really?"

"Originally," said Mercoeur, "I came to Russia as a French footman for the Sheremetev family. Later on, I became the valet de chambre of the young Count Torby, a son produced by the morganatic marriage of Grand Duke Mikhail Mikhailovich with a Countess Merenberg. However, a few months after the outbreak of the revolution, I was ordered to serve the czar. For they had deprived him of his domestics, who were still influenced by the mood of the court, and they made me available to him because they assumed that I shared the sentiments of the populace."

"Indeed," said Maltravers, "they seem to have hit the nail on the head. And you most likely still share the sentiments of the populace, *n'est-ce pas*? Otherwise you would not have butted into our conversation."

"May I request permission," said Mercoeur, "to withdraw?"

"Permission granted," said Maltravers.

"Oh," cried Levasseur, "do stay! Keep talking!"

"Fine," said Maltravers indifferently, "keep talking, for all I care."

Mercoeur was silent for several moments and he appeared to be swallowing something. Finally, he said: "As the gentlemen wish. But I will take the liberty of mentioning things that may be unpleasant to Monsieur le Comte.

"Well, the court, or what was still known as the court, was already constantly being moved around, in order

84

to elude counter-revolutionary elements. Originally, you see, the czar and his family had been confined in Tobolsk. But then they were taken to Pskov. The court procession was under the command of two commissars, Lazarev and Dunin. An infantry division had been detailed to guard the procession. The railroad train consisted of a locomotive and two cars. The first car contained the czar, the czarina, the czarevich, and the grand duchesses Tatyana, Maria, Olga, Anastasia, and the rest of the imperial suite, consisting of the Comptroller of the Imperial Household Countess Stolypin, Cavalry General Cherkasov, and the hunting master Baron Hafferberg. The second car contained the commissars and the soldiers. Initially, the escort had been housed in the first car and the royal household in the second. But since unknown men had tried to uncouple the emperor's car during the journey, the imperial family was rebilleted. All in all, the soldiers were constantly on the alert for attacks and efforts to free the imperial family. Furthermore, during the journey from Tobolsk to Pskov, the peasants knelt by the tracks when the train passed by, and they showed the emperor their old veneration. The commissars did not care for that at all, so they rerouted the transport back to Kazan.

"That was where I joined the transport, along with a female named Anyushka, who had been ordered to serve the empress and the grand duchesses. Anyushka was a lively, indeed sometimes all-too-lively woman. More than anything, she loved joking with the soldiers, and she talked so lasciviously even in the imperial car that the Grand Mistress of the Order of the Holy Martyr St. Catherine began to fear that Anyushka would corrupt even the head of the third hussar regiment of Yelisavetgrad."

"What's he talking about?" asked Levasseur, and Maltravers too gazed in bewilderment at the waiter. But then a moment later, reaching up to the bookshelf overhead, he pulled down a small volume. It was an old court register, and he began leafing through it. Mercoeur watched him silently. "Was I right?" he finally asked with a faint grin.

"Yes," Maltravers said nonchalantly. "The Grand Mistress of the Order of St. Catherine," he turned to Levasseur, "was the czarina, and the head of that hussar regiment was Grand Princess Olga. He means that it was unpleasant for the czarina to have that repulsive creature use foul language in front of the grand princess."

"Quite so," said Mercoeur, nodding in satisfaction. "Otherwise, however, the autocrats of all the Russias seldom expressed their discontent about the circumstances. They lived very modestly and retiringly in their car, but managed to while away the boredom of their journey across the steppes by occupying themselves with any number of things—to be sure, things that were more innocuous than intellectual. Having been relieved of the business of ruling the Holy Russian Empire, which he had done so brilliantly, the Czar of Moscow, Kiev, Vladimir, Novgorod, Astrakhan, Poland, Siberia, Georgia, and Taurian Chersonese had already devoted himself in Tobolsk to chopping wood for hours on end, and during the transport he would assist the cook with his work. Whenever I entered to perform some duty, I found the Grand Prince of Smolensk, Lithuania, and Volynia, the Prince of Estonia, Livonia, Courland, and Semgallen, Samogitia, Carelia, Tver, Yugoria, Permia, and other countries busy peeling potatoes. And the hetman of all the Cossack troops— Monsieur le Comte must know without looking it up that I am referring to the czarevich—was helping him. Their Imperial Highnesses were involved in manual chores that were of no use to anyone, and often the Supreme Rulers remained kneeling for hours on end, praying to the Supreme Being, but their efforts met with no success, for the Lord of Hosts and King of Kings did not come to their rescue."

This man obviously had a titlemania, or at least an astounding memory for titles and persons, which is sometimes the case with people who have a great deal to do with courtly circles and, because they themselves are granted no titles and achieve nothing else, they eventually become revolutionaries after an initially excessive admiration of the higher world. There was something sneeringly sinister, indeed, downright macabre about the way Mercoeur delivered his speech and dug up long-forgotten ranks. Leafing through the court registry, Maltravers satisfied himself that the titles were all correct. He began to feel almost mesmerized by the grotesque narrator, and Levasseur too was listening in extreme suspense.

"The inhabitants of the imperial car," Mercoeur went on, "also enjoyed telling one another stories. The Lord and Grand Prince of Chernigov, Rostov, Yaroslav, Belosero, Udoria, of Novgorod of the Lower Land, of Mtislav and the entire Northern Territory, the Lord and Ruler of the lands of Iveria, Cabardinia, and the Province of Armenia, had proposed the idea, and Princess Stolypin, Comptroller of the Imperial Household and Lady-in-Waiting with the Imperial Portrait joined in, as did Cavalry General Cherkasov. Indeed, sometimes even Commissars Lazarev and Dunin walked in, listened for a while, and then likewise told some little story or other. It was a veritable idyll, for everyone had, as it were, grown accustomed to everyone else. Only

Hunting Master Baron Hafferberg told no stories, for none occurred to him, although he was often supremely asked by the Inheritor and Ruler of the Circassian and Mountain Princes, the Lord of Turkestan, and Heir of Norway. However, Baron Hafferberg came up with absolutely nothing. For he was not exactly a shining light."

All the fantastic titles produced by Mercoeur referred, as Maltravers determined, to the czar. He also noted that when citing the so-called "Grand Title" of the czar, the waiter did not toss everything pell-mell; rather, he followed the prescribed order, and would probably soon be coming to the purely military ranks. The count would not be disappointed. Mercoeur actually knew the entire enormous title by heart.

"However," he continued, "even Hafferberg was gradually seized with the ambition of likewise telling a story. But first, he said, he would have to think one up. And from then on, he sat there, thinking one up.

"Meanwhile the transport was approaching Ufa. According to information that we received by telegraph, our spies had ferreted out that Cossacks of the so-called Golden Horde were planning to attack us near Orenburg. The Cossacks wanted to rip out the tracks, force their way into the train, and free the imperial family. But if the railroad workers noticed that the tracks were ripped out, the train might back up and flee. So two officers of the White troops were to infiltrate our train in order to strike down the engineer and the stoker at the proper moment and take over the locomotive. They were to do so without weapons, for in case of a body search, the two infiltrators must not be armed. The men chosen for this bold venture were Herr von Rosenthorpe and Count Maltravers."

Here, Mercoeur paused and looked at the count. But

the count was gazing into space. "Well?" he at last said casually.

"Rosenthorpe," explained Mercoeur, "was a Russian rittmaster, the son of Torsten von Rosenthorphe from Ingria. Maltravers was not Russian. He had been captured as an Austrian officer in 1915. But in 1918, he declared himself Czech, for he came from some Czech area of Austria. He was released from the prisoner-of-war camp so that he might join the Czech legions. However, he did not do so; instead, he immediately joined the counter-revolutionary troops."

"Jolly decent of him!" said Maltravers. "For he had sworn an oath of allegiance, which he did not break, but kept in his way, by making himself, as a nobleman, available to the czar."

"As Monsieur le Comte wishes," said Mercoeur. "In any case, you see that everything was already revealed and known and was therefore hopeless by the time Rosenthorpe and Maltravers appeared in their previously described garb at the tiny station outside Ufa, whose name, as I have said, I have forgotten. Or does Monsieur le Comte perhaps still recall the name of the station?"

"Come now!" said Maltravers.

"Very good," said Mercoeur, "nor does the name really matter. In any event, we acted as if we were not in the picture, and we welcomed the two peasant gentlemen with a downright hypocritical friendliness. The peasant gentlemen asked if they could go along to Orenburg, and they were naive enough to think that we would really allow them to join us on such an important transport even if we had had no reason to take them along. But we did have a reason, and we took them along. For we wanted to learn from them how far the counter-revolutionary movement had spread among the Cossacks and what else they were planning.

"The peasant gentlemen, as I have said, were carrying chickens. They said that these were their provisions for the journey, but that they were willing to sell the chickens or trade them for something else. The leader of the regiments of the Guards of Preobrashensky, Semyonovsky, Ismailovsky, and Pavlovsky was immediately interested in buying the chickens, for, as czar, he had a fine palate. Nor did Commissar Lazarev basically have anything against the purchase. But since, being an intellectual, he could not stand the sight of blood, although he had already ordered the shootings of quite a number of people and his heart was nurturing a very special project along those lines, he declared that the chickens could be slaughtered only when he was in the other car. And that was what happened. He went over to the troop car, and the chickens were purchased at the Supreme Wish and transported from life to death. That was, no doubt, the final death sentence to be issued and carried out by the old regime.

"On this occasion, the peasant gentlemen tried to whisper something to the Commander of the First Yekaterinoslav Grenadier Regiment of Emperor Alexander III, of the Twelfth Astrakhan Grenadier Regiment, and of the Thirteenth Erivan Grenadier Regiment—all of them the czar, Monsieur le Comte! But the visitors could only manage incoherent hints, for the sentries were always present. However, in an unguarded moment, Maltravers took Baron Hafferberg aside in order to tell him something. But that was an egregious blunder. For the valiant Hunting Master was so profoundly absorbed in thinking up a story and, in general, mentally so ill-equipped that he yelled at the filthy peasant gentleman: What did he want from him anyway! The peasant gentleman thereupon withdrew angrily. *N'est-ce pas*, Monsieur le Comte?

"We, in any case, watched all this, surreptitiously laughing our hearts out. But meanwhile, the Commander of the Forty-Fourth Dragoon Regiment of Nizhny Novgorod, of Emperor Alexander's Royal Prussian Grenadier Regiment of Guards No. 1, and the Commanding Lieutenant of the Royal Great British Dragoon Regiment of Royal Scots Greys (for the czar was even head of that)—meanwhile he had sensed that something was amiss, and he had informed his family, so that a perceptible tension soon became noticeable among the Varangians in the imperial car. Around nine o'clock that evening, the czarina, evidently in her capacity as Commander of Empress Alexandra's Second Ulan Regiment of Guards, of Alexandra Feodorovna's Fifteenth Dragoon Regiment, or the Crimean Cavalry Regiment of the same name, tried to contact Rittmaster von Rosenthorpe, who may have served in one of those regiments. She was represented by Dunin. The latter placed his hand on Rosenthorpe's shoulder. But Rosenthorpe was obviously still too fine to be touched by such a fellow. He forgot his role and struck Dunin in the chest. Thereupon, Dunin, who, unlike his comrade Lazarev, could easily stand the sight of blood, pulled out his revolver and gunned Rosenthorpe down.

"When Maltravers heard the shot, he assumed that everything had come out. He knocked down two sentries, leaped off the train, and was never seen again, at least by me—until today, when I had the pleasure of observing that Monsieur le Comte is still in good health."

"Thank you very much," said Maltravers, unmoved. "I am, of course, someone else, but I am nevertheless in decent health." And he smiled engagingly at Levasseur, who stared at him with gaping eyes.

"We, however," Mercoeur continued, "arrived in Ufa, where we changed our plans completely. We let the train go on to Orenburg, but without us, and there was no one aboard except for the dead Rosenthorpe. Back then, one could indulge in such pranks in Russia. When the train derailed at the ripped-up section of the track, the mounted Cossack troops of the Golden Horde, with lances and banners, must have been quite amazed at the nice surprise. Indeed, they must have been a stupid bunch, those Cossacks! A few years later, when the Soviets launched a census, whole tribes came down from the Caucasian Mountains, and no one had even dreamt that they existed. They still wore harnesses and coats of mail as they had a thousand years ago.

"Well, they may have buried Rosenthorpe. But we loaded our prisoners on two trucks, and off we drove toward the Urals. We stood crowded in among the soldiers, rocking back and forth as we lumbered along; their Supreme Majesties were likewise rocking to and fro, and even the Honorary Admiral of the Royal British, Royal Swedish, and Royal Danish Navies, although he should have been used to such a motion from ships, was swaying so vehemently that all his medals would have collided and clattered, if he had been wearing them: the Spanish Order of the Golden Fleece, the Order of the Elephant, the Order of the Annunciata, the Order of Seraph, the Order of the Garter, and goodness knows what other orders. There was no longer any question of telling stories. For days on end, we drove through the Urals, then along the Chusavaya, arriving in Yekaterinburg on the evening of the third day. Here, we were billeted in an empty house belonging to the merchant Ipatyev, their Supreme Majesties on one side, and we, together with Princess Stolypin, Cherkasov, and Hafferberg on the other. When we gathered in the evening, the mood of the latter three was already quite dejected, and no one really felt like telling stories anymore. We maintained a dignified silence; but all at once, we heard a series of dull detonations from below, evidently from the cellar. Those were the shots, as we presently learned, that had felled the entire imperial family. Now, an utter and deathly hush began, and in that hush, Hunting Master Baron Hafferberg suddenly said he had finally thought of a story, which he would now tell. His lips were actually parting when the door opened wide and Dunin entered, calling for him, Cherkasov, and Princess Stolypin in order to have them shot too. So no one has ever heard the story that Hafferberg went to such great lengths to think up."

And Mercoeur lit the count's cigar, which had gone out; he then bowed and left.

Levasseur sat there speechless for a while, Maltravers also kept silent, and from the other end of the table, they heard the voices of Henrikstein and Lisette Levasseur, who had been chatting with one another all the time and had not even noticed anything of the waiter's tale.

"Listen," Levasseur finally blurted out, "is that true, Count Fortescue? Were you really involved in all that, and what name did that man keep addressing you by?"

"A name?" said Maltravers. "You believe you heard him address me by a different name? Well, perhaps he did. But I have forgotten that name. And perhaps his story is true. But it all took place long ago, and it too has been forgotten long since. Nevertheless, he could really imagine that I am someone other than myself, and he could blab it about and cause us some minor unpleasantries. If you care to take my advice: when you pay the check, tip him a thousand francs to buy his silence. For he must at least know the value of money. You can see that he quit Russia once there was nothing more for him to get out of it. He switched gears and is again taking tips from the bourgeois rabble. What is past is past, dear Monsieur Levasseur. The czar and his family have been dead for a long time, rotting in the so-called Mine of the Four Brothers; only the head of Nicholas II, with a bullet hole in one eye—a dreadful sight to behold—is preserved as *corpus delicti* in a crate at the Kremlin. But the world goes on. We too ought to let the past remain the past. It would do better to focus on these young people, who have meanwhile, I hope, been enjoying a marvelous conversation. *N'est-ce pas*, Edgar?" And he turned to Henrikstein.

Henrikstein looked up, smiled, and said he had spent a delightful hour chatting with Madame. Maltravers now suggested going to a nightclub, but Mme. Levasseur rose abruptly, declaring she had a headache, and asked her husband to take her home.

So they left the Grand Veneur after Mercoeur had received his thousand francs. However, he thanked the count, and not Monsieur Levasseur. But the count pretended not to hear. Out in the street, the Levasseurs said good night after Monsieur Levasseur but not Mme. Levasseur had asked the count and Henrikstein to call on them very soon. Then they got into their automobile.

"An attractive woman," Maltravers said to Henrikstein, watching the automobile drive off. "And you must have made an extraordinary impact on her, Edgar. Otherwise she would not have gotten that headache."

"Do you think so?" said Henrikstein. "By the way, why don't we drop in at the Chapeau Rouge?"

"No," said Maltravers. "We are going to bed. I would like to spend some time alone with you tonight. And besides, after enjoying an evening with such a charming woman, one does not go to a girl like that Lolita."

SEVEN

The next evening, Maltravers again declared that he did not wish to go to the Chapeau Rouge, and likewise the evening after that. But on the third evening, after seeing *Turandot* with the Levasseurs and supping with them (whereupon the Levasseurs drove home), the two men went back to the Chapeau.

The count chatted amiably and sympathetically with Lola, but during the drive home, after humming "Nessun dorma" to himself for a while, he abruptly said to Henrikstein: "You should not get too used to that woman, Edgar. Women are never as they are, they are always only as one sees them. And one always sees them only in such a way as to please oneself. They exist by dint of our deceiving ourselves until we become accustomed to them. A relationship is nothing but habit. But one never grows accustomed to love. You and your lady friend, for example, are happy just to see each other. But people should be able to make each other unhappy rather than happy. In point of fact, love does not strike me as existing in order to make us happy. Nothing that comes from the gods makes us happy. For the gods not only attract, they also reject. You probably do not quite understand that, Edgar, and women do not understand it either. They are usually too practical to let a man become unhappy. They prefer making him happy, and they themselves eventually become indifferent, that is all. In short—what did I want to say?—in short, Lolita is not a lover for you, and you are not meant for her. She ought to marry some day. That would certainly be best. But she cannot possibly interest you any further, and I will never set foot inside the Chapeau Rouge again."

And he leaned back and continued to hum, "No One Shall Sleep!"

Indeed, he never did go back to the Chapeau Rouge. But this made no impression on Henrikstein, who had already gotten together with Lola during the last two afternoons without telling the count; and from then on, the two young people kept meeting daily. Oddly enough, Maltravers did not seem to notice Henrikstein's long absence each afternoon. Nor did he ever ask him where he had been, although he must have guessed the truth. Instead, he acted as if the matter were settled. He was plainly one of those people of whom many existed earlier, and for whom—perhaps because they were so harmonious with themselves—anything they did not like simply did not exist. Or else it could have been merely a sign of old age in the count. . . . In any case, he let Henrikstein go where he pleased, and he kept busy in his own way.

Usually, Henrikstein and Lola met in one of the parks, where, despite the season, couples still sat, kissing very unabashedly on the stone benches, which, adorned with trophies, garlands, and cornucopias, had been designed by great artists for the court of the kings. And since other couples were doing it, the two young people did it too; they chatted and smoked, and they went to the fountains and shallow ponds and fed the fish. And many of the passersby looked at the couple.

"Why do people keep looking at us?!" Henrikstein finally said.

"They're looking at you," said Lola. "You must be used to being looked at."

"No," he said. "They're looking at you. They like you."

"They like you a lot more than me," she said. "They're surprised that you're going with me."

Sometimes they wandered through Paris for hours on end. They loved the small gardens behind the Hôtel de Clermont with their boxtree labyrinths and the terrace with bronze bannisters, the cascades in the park of the Duke de Lauzun, the marvelous flowers in the stands on Place Font-le-Roy. They roamed through the tiny alleys on Mont Saint-Michel, drifted about on the Quai de la Ferraille, and gazed into the Seine, where many other people were likewise standing and spitting into the water. Or else they rode the métro to Saint-Pol, an area that they liked for some reason, even though it was ugly. When darkness came, they entered one of the small cafés or Italian tavernas and drank a few glasses of wine; they sat near the organ at the Lavandière, watching the people dance, or they went to the Rainbow, where a primitive kind of five o'clock tea was served. On the whole, they lived in a very un-Parisian way, while not leading the life of foreigners either. Basically, they were uninterested in Paris, they saw only the trivia, which they liked, and they went about like people who would much rather be in an altogether dif-

99

ferent place. Sometimes, upon returning from an out-
ing, they even doubted that they had been in Paris.
And they never rediscovered certain parts of the city
that they had seen. Ultimately, Paris remained alien to
them. Nor did they speak to anyone else. They sometimes imagined it was a very different city with very different people. And they could never have said precisely where they actually were.

They told one another what they had been doing
since their last meeting, or what they had done earlier,
and little by little they narrated their lives to one
another. However, they told only about unimportant
things, as if everything that had happened previously
was meaningless. Nothing was important to them except what they were to each other. The circumstances
seemed inconsequential to them. Even things that
would have been important were viewed as trivial; for
example, they never cudgeled their brains about anything concerning Maltravers and Henrikstein's odd
situation, although, if Henrikstein thought about it on
his own, it often struck him as unclear. But he viewed it
as irrelevant to his interest in Lola. Nor did it bother
him that she had to spend night after night talking to
strangers at the Chapeau Rouge. Both of them had already done far too unpleasant work to let any of it en-
croach upon their lives. They existed for one another,
nothing else interested them. And they felt a very great
security in existing for one another.

Often they went to a film—they sat cuddling in the
darkness, the way lovers have been cuddling in the
darkness since time immemorial, and they gazed at the
screen, on which repeatedly nothing occurred but
what had occurred in them: love. There was no other
theme. In an era when love was said to exist no longer,
all the films in Paris were about nothing but love.

Whether they took place in London or Mexico, in Berlin or Spain, whether between Gary Cooper and Joan Crawford, between Clark Gable and Jean Harlow, every movie was only about love. Anything else that went on was completely false and untrue; only love was real.

There was always a young man and a young girl, she was always pretty, and he was always equally attractive or looked vaguely like a monkey, but then that was supposed to be attractive anyway. And these couples were always ready to fall in love and get married, as if there were no other possibility. Nor was there any. There were no real complications, no obstacles, no Strindbergian dislikes, nothing. All complications and obstacles came only from the outside, from bandits, policemen, criminal sheriffs, and the like; and then a couple of enemies were shot down and the young people could marry. They had no personal resistance. If there was such resistance in a movie, no one went to see it. Everything had to be very simple. Love, too, had become very simple, as it had been at the start of all things. It was amazing that with all such sums of love, with such a general disposition for marriage, there was never the slightest inner complication between lovers. Not even once. The new generation was either too small or too big, too ordinary or too grandiose—probably both at once. To the generation that had come right after the war, everything had seemed outrageously difficult; but the current generation found everything unwontedly simple. There were no more standards to measure the new human beings according to the sublimity of mankind. They were human beings pure and simple.

For Henrikstein and Lola, too, whatever the couples did on screen was as self-evident as if they were doing it themselves. And that was what they did. They loved one another just like the two stars in each film. Between their love and that of the stars, who themselves were nothing but two in a million, there was ultimately as little difference as between the love of the stars and the love of some gods. For a film may be banal, but love is neither banal nor grand, neither common nor divine, it is simply love, nothing else. Generations had tried to complicate it, and the hierarchies of heaven and earth had attempted to differentiate it within itself. But it took only one generation to make love simple again. No matter how high the feelings of a queen had been placed over those of a little seamstress, they ultimately turned out to be the same feelings. They simply loved. That was all.

Lola and Henrikstein also loved each other as people have loved since the beginning of time: passionately, blindly, and as a matter of course. Sometimes they wanted to forge plans for the future, but they only managed to come up with very vague sketches. They were accustomed to having the future approach them, and they could not resolve to make any plans. They were not the sort of people who have so little to do with life that they can be stronger than life. Life had always been stronger than they. After all, Henrikstein was actually leading a double life. He spent his evenings with Maltravers and the Levasseurs or friends of the Levasseurs, in very exclusive circles to which people who are not Parisians normally have no access. In the daytime, he went his own way, and so did Maltravers.

The count's way was bizarre enough, although he usually wandered only between Ile de la Cité and the Hôtel de Cluny.

For one day, while crossing the Pont Neuf, he had noticed a section of the banks of the Cité: it had reminded him of the terrain he had seen in his dream in the light of the wagon lanterns, when he had been thought dead. He was unable to pinpoint the similarity. Moreover, the dream terrain had been wooded, and here there were only streets, bridges, mansions, and the river. But he suddenly felt as if these buildings were in the enchanted forest and the river were flowing through many trees. This impression had haunted the count until his arrival at the Hôtel de Cluny. There, he lost himself, after a passing Cadillac had let out a strange, lengthy beep, as if a dwarf were blowing his horn.

Ever since, the count had often visited the Hôtel-Dieu, Notre Dame, and the Palais de Justice, and he had the feeling that he had been to those places before, especially when in a short stretch of corridor next to the Salle de Saint-Louis in the Conciergerie; but several paces further, everything seemed unfamiliar again. He also frequently stood in the street din outside the Hôtel de Cluny at the corner of Boulevard Saint-Michel and Boulevard Saint-Germain, and he believed that everything was silent, and only the forest was murmuring around him. . . .

The night of December 24, after they had dined only on Lenten dishes, Maltravers said he wanted to attend midnight mass at the Sainte-Chapelle, and he asked Henrikstein to accompany him.

As they got out of the car and entered the Court of Honor at the Palais de Justice, Maltravers said, "I finally want to hear this mass again in a place where my people used to hear it ever since their christenings. Back then, my people were renowned for their long hair. It was light yellow and knotted behind like the tails of plough horses. Nevertheless, the end of the hair dropped all the way down the back. On the other hand—for who would wear it like that today!—my hair is still rather short. Thus everything balances out." And, walking through the Galerie de la Sainte-Chapelle, he said, "In this building, those long-haired people held the *Lit de Justice*. That was the supreme tribunal. They lay down here in the "Bed of Justice." But I can tell you, my dear Edgar, that the Bed of Justice is not always as softly cushioned as the throne of France."

With these remarks, which Henrikstein must have found utterly incomprehensible, they entered the courtyard of the Sainte-Chapelle. The church was lit inside by candles, and the windows shone like flickering towers in fabulous colors. The interior was filled with people, and Maltravers and Henrikstein, standing in the background, heard the mass. The music was played on an organ, and the singing voices sounded just like the voices of angels who, having descended from the heavens to the ceiling vault, were praising the miracle of the rose that had blossomed in the winter night.

After mass, the two men drove back to the Claridge, and Maltravers ordered white bread and fruit cake, pork, grapes, and some wine. Then he went to bed. But he never resumed his bizarre walks between the island in the Seine and the Hôtel de Cluny.

In mid-January, more or less, when Gomez brought him another one of the mysterious checks from which the count had been living, the agent said:

"Your income is quite considerable now. Do you really spend the money or do you still have it?"

"I have most of it on me," said Maltravers.

"Well, then," said Gomez, "you have capital. You could start something with that. Would you perhaps like to double it?"

"Why not," said Maltravers. "But it would have to

happen in an utterly correct way."

Thereupon, the two men set out on an undertaking that would have been incomprehensible, at least for the count, had it not been consistent with his character to occasionally do something incomprehensible or at least to pay no heed to what he was doing. He simply did not think about it. Or he thought about it too late. He was probably thinking about something else altogether. For instance, it later struck him as quite incomprehensible that he should actually have cheated at cards. But at the time of his cheating, it had evidently not been ratified by his mind. He could also, of course, have done the most admirable things just as easily and in the same way. If it did not suit him, he simply stopped evaluating or adhering to the scales of good or bad. He squandered not only money, but also positions, advantages, and privileges of his person, his own life, and even himself. For he disregarded not only things, but also himself. These mental characteristics, this bizarre absentmindedness of the grand seigneur, these moral intervals of his made him capable of doing many things. Indeed, he was said to be capable of anything. But people who are capable of anything are also capable of nothing. That would be revealed again, here and later. . . .

For now, at any rate, he and Gomez went about their business. Gomez knew a certain Monsieur Flesch, an alleged representative of Schroeder, a jeweler in Amsterdam. They went to see Flesch and examined his jewelry. Gomez noticed a single, very large, pear-shaped rose pearl.

He took his leave and went off with Maltravers, but then rang up Flesch and said, "Sell the rose pearl to Crozet on Rue de la Paix, if necessary below the price."

Flesch, after some difficulties—for Crozet the

jeweler did not wish to buy it—sold him the pearl below its price.

Two days later, Maltravers came to Crozet, inspected various items, and finally pretended to discover the pearl. He claimed he liked it very much. He then bought it, handing Crozet a check.

Crozet turned the check over and over in his hand, stammering that he could give him the pearl only after inquiring whether the check was covered, and his voice, rustling like tissue paper, grew less and less intelligible.

"By all means," said Maltravers magnanimously. "Please hold on to the pearl, and once the check has cleared, please bring me the pearl at the Claridge."

The next day, Crozet cashed the check and brought the pearl to the count with endless apologies.

After that, nothing happened for a while. But then, an apparent mass of anxieties, the count showed up again at Crozet's boutique and declared that the pearl had a companion piece.

"What sort of companion piece?" asked Crozet.

A man named Flesch, said the count, owned a companion piece, a second pearl, which looked identical with the one that he, Maltravers, had bought from Crozet. The two pearls, he explained, were actually from a pair of earrings; he no longer enjoyed having just one, he had to have the second one, too, but Flesch was charging an outrageous price.

Crozet stammered that he had bought the pearl from Flesch, not knowing there was a second one just like it.

"This whole matter," said Maltravers, "is simply an attempt to hoodwink someone!" And he was expressing a great truth.

He begged to differ, said Crozet. For if Flesch had

sold one pearl of the pair, he had only hurt himself. After all, two identical pearls were worth four times as much as a single pearl, and Flesch could not have counted on selling the second pearl as well.

Oh, but he could, said Maltravers. For Flesch had managed to get word to his, the count's, lady friend that a second pearl existed, and this lady friend now wished to own both pearls. Flesch had wanted to earn not four times but six times the price of one pearl.

"Ah," sighed Crozet, "just like a woman!"

"No," said Maltravers, "just like a jeweler! But I have to have the second pearl. That lady keeps tormenting me day and night."

"At night, too?" asked Crozet.

"Of course!" cried Maltravers, glaring at him. For he evidently did not wish to play the fool even in regard to a mistress who did not exist. "In any case," he continued, "you are now obligated to get me the second pearl as cheaply as possible!"

"I?" cried Crozet.

"Yes, you! For it was you who palmed the first one off on me. Flesch is demanding an exorbitant price for the second one. But he will probably let you have it for less, since you are, allegedly, a jeweler, too."

Crozet thereupon resolved to buy the second pearl come what may.

Maltravers left and handed the pearl over to Gomez, and Gomez handed it over to Flesch. When Crozet now came and saw it, he would have to believe that there was truly a second pearl.

When the time was ripe, Maltravers said to Henrikstein:

"Edgar, how are you and Mme. Levasseur getting along?"

"What do you mean, count?"

"Well, said Maltravers, "I mean that as I mean it. The woman is in love with you, is she not?"

Henrikstein lowered his eyes to the floor and said he had almost the same impression. He had to admit it.

"What about you?" asked Maltravers.

"Excuse me?"

"What do you think of her? Do you not find her attractive?"

"Certainly," said Henrikstein.

"Well then!"

Henrikstein looked at him diffidently.

"Do you like her?" asked Maltravers.

"Basically, yes."

"Have you told her so?"

"No."

"Why not?"

"How could I?!"

"It would certainly delight her."

"Do you think so?"

"Definitely! Why have you not done so?"

"Oh," said Henrikstein, "I haven't had the occasion."

"On the contrary," said Maltravers, "you have had every occasion. The interest she shows in you obligates you. You ought to tell her a few things that she would enjoy. It would at least be polite of you. The world may have become impolite, but I would still expect politeness from you. And then, rumor has it that her marriage is on the rocks. But she holds it sacred nonetheless. At least, give her the pleasure of showing her that you are a bit interested in her, and that you are unhappy about having to respect her as another man's wife. Grant her the satisfaction of being admired by you, all the more, because she would never make up her mind to be unfaithful to her husband."

"Do you think so?" asked Henrikstein sheepishly.

"Of course!" said the count. "I will see to it that Mme. Levasseur invites you to tea by yourself. And you will go and make up for the sweet nothings that you have fallen behind in!"

EIGHT

After this conversation, Henrikstein was in an awkward predicament. He was not really interested in Mme. Levasseur. But he admired Maltravers far too greatly to dare throw his chivalrous advice to the winds. So Henrikstein went to have tea with Mme. Levasseur.

Monsieur Levasseur was not present. Henrikstein at first chatted with Lisette. This was followed by a silence, in which one could hear the red tapers crackling on the mantelpiece. The entire house was still, there was plainly no one in the adjacent rooms, and in that stillness Henrikstein kissed Mme. Levasseur. He looked at her and his face slowly moved toward hers, and she looked back at him with gaping eyes, then he kissed her, and she lifted her arms, placed them around his neck, and kissed him back. He could feel her trembling, and he thought to himself that he had behaved chivalrously. But she did not release him, she kept kissing him over and over. She had not wanted to deceive her husband, although she had realized that after all these years of wedlock, he was beginning to feel indifferent toward her and growing interested in other women. Above all, however, she had not dared to cheat on him, because, coming from a humble background, she had no fortune of her own. She was afraid he might throw her out. But when she saw Henrikstein, she lost her head, if only because of his beauty, but primarily because she considered him extremely noble, since he was always with the count. She had an ominous foreboding. But for weeks now, Henrikstein had been acting as if he did not notice that she was falling more and more deeply in love with him. Yet when he kissed her, everything gave way in her, all the caution and composure that she had maintained; she wound her arms around his neck, buried her face in his shoulder, and had difficulty choking back a sob. Basically, she was a poor creature. Had she remained in her own milieu, she might have found happiness. But ever since marrying Levasseur, she had constantly sensed that it would end unhappily—one more reason, incidentally, for finally doing the very thing she feared most. She simply gave in, losing her head and pulling him down to her, and Henrikstein, leaning over her, told himself that she really was an attractive woman.

At that instant, a chair fell over somewhere.

Henrikstein straightened up and, after a moment, walked into one adjacent room and then the other, but found nobody. When he returned, Mme. Levasseur was sitting there, pressing her handkerchief to her lips and staring at him with eyes that were bathed in tears.

"Who," asked Henrikstein, "could that have been?"

She seemed not to understand what he was saying.

"Didn't you hear something like a chair fall over?" he asked.

No, she said, she had heard nothing. She gazed at

him with an incomprehensible and confusing expression; he took a cigarette from the table, but then put it back, murmuring that he would have to go. He wiped away the lipstick.

Lisette did not respond for a while, but at last she stood up.

"Do you really," she asked, "have to leave?"

"Yes," he said, "I think so. Did you really not hear something?"

"No," she said.

And a moment later, she shook his hand and said: "Please go!"

On the way home, he was annoyed about what had happened. It was unlikely, but nevertheless possible, that someone had observed them without being heard; someone could have opened a door and then immediately retreated, knocking over a chair. Actually, it did not interest Henrikstein. After all, Lisette did not interest him. Then why did he feel so blue? Not that he would have found it disagreeable to be unfaithful to Lola. Among people as simple as they, there was no unfaithfulness in such a luxurious sense. He loved Lola and she loved him, nothing else mattered to either of them. Nevertheless, he had a very unpleasant feeling, which he was at a loss to understand. He decided to apologize to Mme. Levasseur the next day, in order to clear up the entire incident. He then went to her home but was not received.

While Henrikstein was out, Gomez came to see Maltravers at the Claridge. He brought him a great deal of money. Crozet had repurchased the pearl from Flesch at a price far above its value, and the agent was bringing the count the profit minus his own and Flesch's commissions.

"Well?" he asked. "Happy? Everything is quite correct. The law can't get you."

"Crozet," said Maltravers, "rang me up the moment he bought the pearl. How much? I asked. He gave me the price, which was even higher than the actual price. Evidently, he had already added his markup. I instantly became rather aloof and said that his price was really a bit too high, and he grew nervous and said he would be willing to resell me the pearl at a slight loss, for he himself was not interested in it and had only bought it as a favor for me and so on. He wanted to bring it over right away. The situation was plainly making him squeamish. But I said I had no time and told him to come the next morning. Finally he said that my order had been binding. But I said I had not bound myself in any way, of course. I had merely stated that I wanted to have the pearl but had not committed myself to any price. We would see tomorrow. And at that point, even though he was retorting something and screaming into the telephone, I could have hung up, and everything would have been in order. He would have come tomorrow, would not have found me," said Maltravers, counting the money that lay on the table, "and would have lost eighty-three thousand francs. Just as I was putting down the receiver, I changed my mind. I raised the receiver to my ear again, Crozet's agitated voice was still on the telephone, and I told him he might as well come today. He was here fifteen minutes ago, and I bought the pearl from him again."

Gomez thought he was hearing things.

"Pardon me?" he stuttered. "What did you buy from him?"

"The pearl. For one hundred thirty thousand francs."

"For! . . ." shouted Gomez. "The pearl?"

"Yes," said Maltravers. "Here it is." And he produced

it from his trouser pocket and tossed it on the table. It bounced up from the wood, struck it again, trundled unevenly over the edge of the table, and fell to the carpet.

Gomez gaped alternately at the pearl and at the count.

"Don't," he finally blurted out, "be funny."

"I am not," said Maltravers, and while Gomez, aghast, picked up the pearl, the count added: "Please be so kind as to resell it for me. You will most likely obtain a third or a quarter of the money."

"But my God," cried Gomez, "have you gone insane? Why did you do it?"

"All at once," said Maltravers, "it struck me as very unfair to hoodwink Crozet."

"What do you mean!" shouted Gomez, "You said it should all be done correctly. And everything *was* perfectly correct! No one could have called you to account, you poor man!"

"Exactly," said Maltravers. "For 'correct' is worth something. But it would not have been fair. Most of the crimes that are committed are, officially, correct actions. The laws themselves cover nearly all skillfully perpetrated crimes. Only crimes committed in a primitive manner are punished. I personally know that better than anyone else. . . . Had I, say, stolen money from the common people instead of cheating at cards, I would have been awarded a Commander Cross. No, Gomez, correctness is no yardstick. One must be fair. We have to answer to ourselves, not to the law. That is the point. And I personally would have considered it irresponsible to bilk Crozet."

"Ah," said Gomez, "but he's such a jackass!"

"Jackass or not," said Maltravers, "I will not even bilk a jackass."

"I see!" shouted the agent. "And that was why we ran our legs off!"

"Stop shouting, Gomez," said Maltravers. "And stop exciting yourself. You ought to have foreseen that I would not ultimately carry it through. After all, I did tell you that I have become moral."

"No. You said you wanted to be correct! You yourself feel there is a distinction. What would become of people otherwise!"

"Come now," said Maltravers, "admit that you could not steal money from anyone's pocket in an incorrect way. But I said I wanted to be fair."

"Oh, my goodness," cried Gomez, "you are growing more difficult by the minute! Next you'll be telling me you'd like to be a saint!"

"That would be going too far," said Maltravers. "I am not passionate enough to repent my sins rather than commit them. But let us forget about that. Please just resell the pearl for me and send me the money. In any case, let us drop the matter. . . . My sole regret is that we must now part company, Gomez. I was just growing used to you again."

"Yes," said Gomez, "and I'll miss you too, even though you've played this trick on me. You can't afford to do such things, Maltravers! Actually, I wonder whether I ought to leave you alone. What good are the best ideas if you don't carry them out! Everything is all arranged for the next case. But are you going to go on strike again?"

"No," said Maltravers after a moment. "I cannot suddenly drop the boy. Incidentally, did I not say that it is unnecessary to tell him the truth?"

"I must admit you did. And are you satisfied with him otherwise?"

"Oh, goodness, fairly, even though ultimately there

is something about him that alienates me. After all, his background is so utterly different from mine. Or perhaps the young people of today are generally such that we no longer understand them. We—not just I, but you, too, Gomez, although your father was a mule driver—we were never truly free. We always served a world that could perhaps be described as highly privileged, but it was our world all the same. We were somehow men of the world. A man of the world is not a man who goes out into the world, but a man who is worldly. People today, however, are no longer worldly in any way. They serve no one. They are free. Perhaps they may soon be worldly again. Indeed, most likely. After all, worlds come and go. But, for the time being, they have no world. For a while, I even thought Edgar a proletarian. But he is not one. Proletarians are people who are expelled from a world even if they rule it. But a real world no longer exists anymore, and neither do any real proletarians. On the other hand, they say that young people now adhere to certain ideas. Ideas are the happiness of the individual and the unhappiness of the collective. But I believe that the individual no longer feels this happiness and the collective no longer feels this unhappiness. The boy is nothing but a young man, and that Lolita, whom he meets every day, is nothing but a young woman. . . . The two of them simply exist. They do not understand why they should not exist for one another. I must admit that I could not talk him into giving her up. I must content myself with a state of affairs that at least does not disturb me. I simply have no real influence on this generation. Perhaps this generation is right and I am wrong. The century is always right. The present is always right. The present is divine. The moment is the only time in which the gods reveal themselves. All reality,

117

too, is divine, and the divine is always quite simple. There is no difference between a mythical love between gods and the simplicity with which two young people of today meet in Montmartre. We, dear Gomez, were actually a quite unreal generation. We had very poor relations with the gods. For us, they were the hopeless remoteness. People today know nothing about them, but they have regained everything that humanity takes for granted. Only the human is divine. There are no other gods. I believe you no longer fully understand me, Gomez, *n'est-ce pas?*"

"That's right," said Gomez. "Recently, your words have become as foolish as your actions, and I really can't follow you. Besides, I have never been concerned about such things. And everything should probably be quite different."

They fell silent, gazing at each other for a long time. Eventually, Gomez, somewhat unsure of himself, said he would have to be going. In any case, he would resell the damned pearl. And standing up, he shook hands with Maltravers.

"Farewell," said Maltravers, "and I wish you the very best, Gomez! We have already met twice. Perhaps we will meet a third time. Unless in the meantime, you. . . . " And he motioned politely toward the floor and the sky, adding: "As you like."

"You're terrible," said Gomez. "And you're not even thinking about yourself?"

"Oh, but I am," said Maltravers. "Only I believe that I shall allow you to precede me. For we have such opposite wishes for ourselves. I want to die, and you do not. Destiny will disappoint both of us. But you shall see: the other world has its charms. In any case: go with God, you old rascal!" And he patted him on the back.

"Yes," said Gomez, "and you too, you old rascal—al-

118

though you suddenly imagine that you're a man of honor—go with God!"

And they separated, laughing, although both of them were a bit sad.

A brief time later, Henrikstein came in. His face was pale and he was clutching an opened letter, which he wordlessly handed to the count.

The letter was from Mme. Levasseur, and it tersely said that she considered Henrikstein a scoundrel.

Maltravers glanced at the letter, then looked up and asked: "Did you call on her yesterday?"

"Yes," said Henrikstein, "and the scene you so greatly wished for developed. I wanted to go back today and apologize, but I was not received, and when I came home, I found this letter."

Maltravers turned the letter back and forth in his hands. Finally he tossed it on the table and said: "A hysterical female, that is all!"

"When we kissed," said Henrikstein, "I heard a chair toppling in the next room. But Mme. Levasseur didn't hear anything—she said."

"You even kissed her?" said Maltravers. "Well, a woman whom you kiss has indeed nothing else to hear or see, my dear Edgar."

"Do you think someone noticed it, count? Maybe it caused her some trouble. But why would she consider me a bad person? She must have sensed that the scene suddenly became embarrassing enough for me! I don't understand the whole business."

"Nor do I," said Maltravers. "But that has nothing to do with the matter, and there is no need for you even to react. You will probably never see Lisette Levasseur again. We are leaving Paris. Tomorrow morning we are going to Rome."

Maltravers offered some flimsy reasons for this sudden departure, but his excuses said as little as his usual comments when he talked about something for a quarter of an hour without really saying anything about it. In any case, the trip was no mere whim. His mind seemed firmly made up. His decision was evidently based on some private motives, and Henrikstein did not have the slightest idea of the count's affairs.

Henrikstein was more than miserable at having to part from Lola. This was the first time after a period of apparent freedom that he felt the shackles binding him to Maltravers. For a moment, he considered staying on in Paris, but then instantly rejected the idea. He would have been left in a far more wretched condition than when the count had found him. He decided, at least for now, to accompany him to Rome.

That evening, he went to the Chapeau Rouge alone. He said goodbye to Lola, and she wept terribly. Later, her boss scolded her. He said she was supposed to laugh with the men, not cry. But she had really wept. Simple women can still shed genuine tears at weddings, funerals, and departures, when others merely want to put the situation behind them.

Henrikstein said he would look about in Rome to see whether he could find Lola a job in a review or something similar.

Before leaving, he got engaged to her.

NINE

Maltravers and Henrikstein spent several hours in Milan, because the count had some business, which he did not go into. Meanwhile, Henrikstein sat in a café, trying to write a letter to Lola. He meant to write a long, real letter, but he couldn't. No one can write the "real." So he merely wrote that he loved her, but after writing it, he felt that it said nothing. It was not crucial. There was something more inevitable about his relationship to her. Love is not inevitable. Life is far more inevitable. It decides on every relationship.

Maltravers also wrote something while still at the railroad station: a long telegram to a Frau von Liebenwein in Vienna, as Henrikstein saw. When they continued their journey, the count chatted with Henrikstein almost the entire evening, again thoroughly enchanting the young man, who had already grown half aloof toward him.

"Are you sorry," asked the count as the train raced through Lombardy with a steady hum, "are you sorry to be away from Paris? You should not be sorry. Tears are being shed for you. . . . For example, by Mme. Levasseur, despite the crazy letter she wrote you. She hates you, but hate is actually the form of love for which one sheds the most tears. There is nothing like love to make us feel we have missed out on so much. But it is far worse to have missed out on hate. Still, be that as it may, you have departed. One must be able to depart if one wishes to live. Returning is almost death. I returned somewhere only once in my life and it was almost the death of me."

Falling silent, he pensively scrutinized his hands in thick beige suede gloves with stitched-on seams. Dusk was already settling in, and in order to see his gloves more sharply, he brought them up to his eyes and examined the seams. Then he folded his hands in his lap again. The gloves gave him an air of being extraordinarily dressed, almost armed. Finally, he leaned back and gazed at Henrikstein. While the count had been speaking, the young man had been looking out the window; now he stared at the floor, but then his eyes suddenly darted up. In the twilight, his gaze, surrounded by a gloriole of long, dark lashes, sparkled momentarily with azure fire, almost like the eyes of a woman, but then dropped again, as if shot down. Maltravers smiled. A man wearing a uniform came through the sleeping-cars, opening the compartments, switching on the light, and announcing that dinner was served. Maltravers stood up and, followed by Henrikstein, went to the dining-car. While the two of them sat, facing each other, at a table with a lamp shining through a red shade, the count, playing with some olives and tuna fish on his plate, said, "To leave, my dear Edgar, and not come back—that is the ticket! But women never want to let a man leave, not because they care for him, but because they know a lot more about life than we do, and because it is dangerous for them if we live it. Even if they have experienced nothing, they still know more about life than we, even if we have experienced everything. They are so close to life that it is no longer a sensation for them, but merely a competition. For they operate with the same devices as life. Nevertheless, life is stronger than they. It never restores to them anyone whom they have lost to it. Eventually they hate it so intensely that they actually forgo having their own experiences. An experience means everything to a man, but basically not much to a woman. Women can get along without experiences. They themselves are experiences. They are dependent on men who have no experiences. Perhaps you were an experience for the Levasseur woman. You most likely were. She was unable to keep playing her role."

And lighting a cigarette, he blew the smoke on the meat that had been served to him.

"Naturally," he went on, "it is always very bad when the woman comes out in a woman. But do not let it get to you. With every woman who gives a man up, the world lies at his feet again. The life of Paris and Rome bows before you, the girls of England and the women of America are yours if you are but free for them. The whole glory of life lies ahead of you. For life means: conquering. And today one need no longer be a prince if one wishes to conquer. A man only has to be something like you. Today, one conquers people, not countries. In earlier days, people would not let themselves be vanquished. But today's people can easily be brought to their knees. Nor are countries captured with ships and armies, people are vanquished through themselves. Attica and the islands floating in the blueness of the ocean, the feasts in the hotels of Egypt, the

123

fairy tales of Bagdad and Babylon, the South Seas and all the creatures of the earth, the wonders of the world, they are yours if you only take them. Incidentally, the food here is terrible! Do you not agree, Edgar?" And telling the waiter to remove the course, he ordered chops with green peas. "But what," he then asked, "was I going to say? What was I talking about? Life? Yes, I think so. A hero's life today is a campaign of Alexander the Great, much further than India. The hero is the man who does not turn back. One should never turn back. For what is past is past. All bygones are death. Only the moment is life, only the future is the gods. They have graced you with everything they can lavish. Supposedly, their gifts are dangerous and corrupt the ones they love. But I believe that they hate only the minions who disappoint them. One must be able to challenge the gods if they are to remain gracious. That is the gist of it! I have challenged them all my life, and I have disappointed them only once, out of weariness. But they do not put up with weariness. They are the never weary. They brought me to the edge of death and showed me the grief of the gray asphodel meadows in the twilight of the netherworld. The beings who live forever will punish with death. They know of no harsher punishment. But they are mistaken. Death is not a punishment. Those who meet with death are already familiar with it. For anyone who is not constantly prepared to die cannot possibly live. Men are more heroic than gods. Life in death was easy for me, too. I often yearn for it. But I am old. You, however, are still very young. It would make no sense for me to teach you experience. Experience only causes anxiety. Nor can I tell you *how* to live. I can only tell you that you *should* live. You should do nothing but live. Life will come to you of its own accord and tempt you. It is a continual temptation. Squander yourself! Life means squandering. I have squandered my entire life, I can leave you nothing from it, but I can be your tempter and show you the splendors of the world, which will fall to its knees and offer itself to you, so that you too will squander it. You shall be my heir."

The next day, around nine o'clock, they arrived in Rome. The morning air was filled with a damp freshness that promised spring. The fountains murmured in the piazzas, the gardens were fragrant with yew, the wind wafted from the sea, and the sacred hills rose into the silvery blue sky.

Maltravers took Henrikstein to the Grand Hotel, not without carping at it because of its useless luxury. They had breakfast on an open terrace in dazzling sunshine. Then they drove to the Forum around lunchtime, spending an hour or two there, smoking cigarettes. There were many other people at the Forum—idlers, beggars, women and children, sitting or lying on the warmed marble and squinting into the sun. Now and then, a gentle breeze carried down the scent of flowers and aromatic herbs from the Palatine, and chestnut oaks and laurel bushes stood tall and silent against the glassy sky. Blue shadows fell from the Capitoline Hill, slowly edging closer. The din of the city was muffled; otherwise this area was almost like the country. A dog barked once or twice, and sometimes the playing children screamed. Yes, it was almost like the country.

At the beginning of time, there had been a swamp here, perhaps even a pond, surrounded by whispering reeds and covered with drifting water lilies; long, long ago, when Italy was still a damp, wooded peninsula teeming with wildlife, stags and wild bulls, bears and lions, and with a few Etruscan castles looming from towns. Then a lost troop of armed young men had come from somewhere in the north, thrown up a ring wall on the Palatine, and worshiped flaxen-haired gods on the Capitoline Square amid the soughing of the two oak groves, where the Palazzo Caffarelli had stood until just recently and where Santa Maria in Araceli now stands. The gods they worshiped may have been Tyr and Donner, although entirely different gods were dwelling there—but the newcomers nevertheless thought that these were their gods. And they had brought the encircling hills under their sway, but they had not even had women as yet; they had still to carry some off. And where the swamp had been, a cattle market gradually developed; and on the flank of the Palatine, peasant vestal virgins established a convent, and tended a sacred fire as they had once done at home in the damp mountain forest, which was swathed in fog. And the cattle market became a Forum, and the tribunes came, and the consuls and the emperors. And again armed men came from the north, the emperors left, and Rome crumbled, and the Forum became a cattle market again. From the dust of a fallen Rome, the ground rose thirty feet higher between the hills, and the forest came again, wild waters roared as in the past, and the aristocracy built tremendous peel towers from the ruins of the ancient monuments. And the towers crumbled, and the cattle market was revived. Then a new breed of men came, excavated the Forum, and planted laurel and flowers amid the marble remnants; idlers basked in the sun, the playing children screamed, sometimes a dog barked, and it was the country again.

Maltravers looked weary and at times he seemed to be dozing. But toward three o'clock, he tossed away his dead cigarette, stood up, knocked the dust from his coat, and adjusted his hat. Then, hanging his cane from his arm, he abruptly said that they had to go buy a car.

They visited several dealerships, and Maltravers, with a dreamy expression on his face, listened to the speeches of the salesmen hawking their cars, while Henrikstein poked around in the vehicles. Since Maltravers never responded, the dealers usually concluded their lectures by offering him a certain discount, whereupon Maltravers nodded, wordlessly left the premises, and Henrikstein, climbing out of the car he was sitting in, followed the count. However, Maltravers's apparent abstractedness was nothing more than his way of concealing his boundless distaste for haggling. "I could," he said to Henrikstein as they walked from one dealership to the next, "more readily rob a man than force him to lower his prices." The count then made a few pejorative remarks about streamlines, declaring that he would not ride in such automobiles. At the final dealership, he did not even allow the salesman to speak. He walked over to a middle-sized car, tapped his cane on the radiator, and asked the price. The salesman asked him to please not tap on the car. Maltravers now tapped his foot rapidly and told the salesman to please be quick and tell him the price. While talking, the count pulled a handful of money from his pocket. The salesman figured he was dealing with a lunatic, who might get away from him, so he quickly told him the price. Maltravers paid out the money on the table, signed a bill of sale and an insurance policy, and said that the car, together with a license plate, was to be outside the "unpleasant" Grand Hotel tomorrow morning at eleven. And he left the dealership. Henrikstein tried to point out that this or that had been forgotten, but was waved off with the comment that nothing had been forgotten, and he,

127

Maltravers, had owned automobiles that were very different from such a "jalopy." And he added, "If it does not run, I will simply hitch oxen to it. After all, way back when, we used to do a great deal of traveling in oxcarts."

Henrikstein did not understand, but the automobile was delivered the next day, and Maltravers got in around twelve noon and told Henrikstein to take the wheel. Turning toward him almost full face and leaning his chin on his hand and his arm on the support, the count pensively gazed at him up close, watching him drive, as if they were in a room and not on the road, and as if he were watching him write, or something of the sort, rather than drive. Henrikstein was a rather bad driver. But Maltravers criticized nothing. His mind was clearly elsewhere.

First they visited a Monsieur des Essarts, a Frenchman who had settled in Rome. That is: Maltravers visited him, while Henrikstein remained downstairs in the car. Then, in order to break the car in slowly on long drives, the count chose the Via Appia. It was dreadfully bumpy; the Roman paving was still there, and it had grown a lot bumpier since ancient days; but Maltravers insisted on driving up and down this thoroughfare, and as they were being shaken to a frazzle on their seats, he stared thoughtfully at the graves decaying by the side of the road. For two days, they drove like that on the Appian Way, constantly outstripped by American and English cars, until Henrikstein silently cursed the road like nothing else in the world, and the count at last declared that the car was broken in.

Aside from his interest in the graves, Maltravers had had no other intention than to drill Henrikstein the way one drills recruits. Otherwise, he would have felt he was losing his grip on him. But the two days of rattling had angered the young man rather than disciplined him. Indeed, he belonged to an undisciplined generation, besides which he had, for years, been down and out, yet completely independent, and he was finding his growing dependence on Maltravers more and more disagreeable, except at those times when the count once again completely enchanted him in some way. While continuously driving up and down the Via Appia and frowning and glaring at its dreadful surface, he began to wonder if he really needed to go on catering to the whims of an old fool. Had he possessed any kind of wherewithal, he would never even have left Paris. But he did not have a sou to his name. Maltravers did give him an allowance, as much as he wanted, but, for decency's sake, he really could not use it to act against the man who gave it to him. However, he did ask himself whether there was no way that he might come to money on his own. He remembered the times when he had often earned as much as several thousand francs for a single fight. Then, of course, the years of breakdown had come. But now, after a few months of complete recovery, he might, if the count's theory was correct, perhaps think about going back to the ring, or at least start his training. He was surprised that Maltravers had not himself suggested it long ago. But Henrikstein decided to bring it up all the same, which he did just as they were getting out of the car the evening of the second day of their horrible drives.

However, Maltravers completely rejected the idea. At first, he merely waved it off, and it was only when Henrikstein grew more insistent that the count asked whether this wish was the sole advantage that Henrikstein had gained from the past few months, and whether nothing better had crossed his mind in Parisian society than "having some mindless opponent smash his mug." This, the count went on, seemed to be the eternal wish of the Germans. Life in Rome was waiting for him, said the count, and any thought of boxing was ludicrous. He could make a very different career for himself, and was he so devoid of imagination that he could not see it? If he absolutely needed some exercise, then he could train a little. But prizefighting was out of the question.

The count thereupon went up to his room. During dinner, he made a few derogatory remarks about professionals, fees, and work in general. Work, he said, was meted out by people who had the power to do so, to other people who were never allowed to come into their own. If he, Henrikstein, were to work, he would never come into his own. Henrikstein wondered why Maltravers was towing him about in the world, but hit on no answer. He finally ascribed it to the count's spleen. Apparently this spleen kept growing. Maltravers, clearly, needed to have only one person around on whom to let out his fits of paradoxical chattiness whenever they overcame him, and which alternated with periods of total muteness. For otherwise it would have been ridiculous to keep anyone like a secretary, since no letters were ever written. The count never wrote a single one. Never. Nor did he receive any. He made fun of letters. He had once told a story about a Hungarian nobleman who for years rented two hotel rooms, one to live in, and the other exclusively for the purpose of throwing in all the mail he received, unopened. When he died, they found the whole room bursting with letters. It was unclear to Henrikstein why people who never received any answers could have written him so many letters. But Maltravers explained that that was precisely the reason why they kept writing. For one writes a real letter only if one is certain that it will never reach the addressee or, at least, that he will not read it. Actually, a letter is addressed to no one. And at that moment, the count looked as if he sometimes wrote such letters himself.

However, Henrikstein did not cudgel his brain about it. The next day, he hired a trainer, an Englishman named Gauntlett, and he then worked out with him for several hours every morning. Maltravers seemed to ignore this, just as he had ignored Lola. Evidently, he did not stop to consider that some private undertaking of Henrikstein's might ultimately disturb him, Maltravers, or run counter to his plans, and he seemed so unconcerned that at times Henrikstein began to have doubts about himself. It appeared that Maltravers truly had the ability to make things he did not like nonexistent. Now and then, he also had a way of looking at people as if they simply did not exist. Had he been a sovereign, he could have annihilated with looks that did not deign to see. But in this way, it remained a mere avocation.

TEN

Early one morning, a week after their arrival in Rome, Maltravers drove alone to the railroad station in order to pick up Marie Liebenwein.

With a cigar in a strange holder made of paper and a quill in his mouth, he drove slowly through the streets, parked at the terminal, and then paced up and down on one of the platforms as he waited for the train, chewing the quill and occasionally twisting it back and forth.

This Frau von Liebenwein was the widow of an extremely distant relative of the Maltraverses. Originally a chambermaid, she had profited from her good looks, making a nice career for herself; ultimately, in a house of very ill fame, where she had played a prominent role, she made the acquaintance of Liebenwein and become his mistress, until he married her, to the displeasure of his family and to the delight of Georg Maltravers. At his death, however, he left her very little. She once again depended on a case-by-case procurement of business that fitted in with her profession, and

Maltravers had likewise availed himself of her services from time to time, although for purposes very different from her normal ones. For she was extremely serviceable in other ways as well. Now she was an old lady who looked like a duchess. For when truly attractive and beautiful people grow old, they only get better looking. She also behaved so astonishingly well in society that no one who did not know could have guessed what she had been earlier. But no sooner was she alone or in an environment where she did not have to practice self-restraint than she became profoundly and poignantly vulgar. Friends who knew her from before would often laugh until tears came to their eyes. Maltravers, however, had always been fairly strict with her.

Nevertheless, when the train arrived and the marvelous-looking old lady got out along with other passengers, she instantly said to Maltravers: "You old codger! I really thought you were moldering in the grave! Glad you're not! It's really great seeing you! You sure are one tough cookie! If ever you kick the bucket, they'll have to shoot you just to make sure!"

"Marie," said Maltravers sedately, as if addressing a domestic who had forgotten herself, "I have, I believe, told you often enough that you are not to get chummy with me in private. You are to use the familiar form only in company. Otherwise, you are to address me as 'Herr Count.' This has not been altered in any way by my death. I do not, to be sure, set any store by my title, I am merely intent on maintaining form. One simply cannot get along without form, Marie. People may do so more frequently today, but in earlier times it would have been utterly impossible. You should know that better than anyone else. Also, you are to express yourself more elegantly about my demise. Incidentally, did you tell anyone where you were going and to whom?"

"Of course not."

"Then we can go," said Maltravers, turning toward the exit.

"Herr Count," said Frau von Liebenwein, "is still as pompous as Herr Count always was."

"Do not think me unfriendly," said Maltravers. "I would like to tell you that I too am delighted to see you again, and I wanted to ask you how you are and how your trip was. But your lack of breeding prevented me from doing so. Do you have a great deal of luggage? Yes? We will send for it later on. And we will take the hand baggage along in the car."

"Herr Count has a car again?"

"Yes."

"How'd you finagle that?"

"I did not finagle it, I purchased it," said Maltravers, as they walked into the square outside the terminal. "But let us save that for later. I have to give you a few more instructions before we reach the hotel." And he opened the car door and helped her in. The hand baggage was stowed away, then he started the car. He again drove very slowly, speaking to her most of the way and occasionally making some kind of explanatory gesture with his right hand. She listened very closely, in the manner of people who definitively register what they are taking in; and, nodding now and then, she said: "Yes indeed, I understand."

"That is good," he said. Now they lapsed into silence; he kept his eyes on the road, driving faster, and she gazed at him thoughtfully. Finally, they pulled up at the hotel; he got out, threw away his cigarette holder, and helped her from the car.

Henrikstein was up in their suite again after his workout.

"This is Herr Henrikstein," said Maltravers. "Frau

von Liebenwein is my cousin and she is affording us the pleasure of her visit for a while, so that we need not always sit around without a lady when we are alone. Would you like to take a nap, Marie, or do you wish to breakfast with us?"

Frau von Liebenwein said she had slept very well in the *couchette*. For she was not high-strung. Women of ill repute are seldom high-strung. They cannot afford to be. Our nerves have a peculiar characteristic: we feel them only if we can allow ourselves to feel them.

So they immediately went down to breakfast. Frau von Liebenwein glanced only casually at Henrikstein. She was still not interested in men who were young and attractive. Indeed, she had gradually become repelled by men in general. She knew them too well. By nature, she was very common, but also quite restrained, like all simple, down-to-earth women, for whom the true intentions of men are merely bad habits, which one must endure every now and then for purely economic reasons. Had she married young and more or less well, she would have become one of the most respectable of women.

Henrikstein looked at her, but she did not look at him again, and he had the slight malaise that a man feels chiefly with young women when he sees that they know all too well what they want: namely, something entirely different. But in this case, he could not, of course, explain his impression, for he really thought that Frau von Liebenwein was a relative of the count's, and indeed her behavior was excellent. Maltravers made small talk, about various visits he was planning and about his acquaintanceship with that Monsieur des Essarts, who was kind enough to wish to introduce the count's entourage into Rome's high society.

While they were still at breakfast, Des Essarts then

appeared in person, returning the count's visit. He was short, slight, and somewhat younger than Maltravers, but, as it turned out, he suffered ever so slightly from flight of ideas. Yet there were people who claimed he did not really suffer from that ailment, but merely pretended to have a poor memory in order to avoid recalling certain irregularities that he had once perpetrated. For example, rumor had it that while gambling, he had taken in the wagers or winnings of other players as if they were his own. For a time, people overlooked his actions because they were too embarrassed to confront him. But when he was finally confronted, he blamed it on his pathological absentmindedness. Indeed, he had always played his role preparatorily. And since he was related by blood or marriage to several great families in France and Italy, people actually did think that he was merely very absentminded. Moreover, although he knew everybody, he pretended to confuse people with one another, and perhaps he really did confuse them, expanding a natural condition purely to his own ends. For he was always pursuing some end or other.

At the moment, incidentally, he was not absentminded, apparently because the matter at hand was important for him too. You see, he was asking the count, Frau von Liebenwein, and Henrikstein to a party at his home next Friday, but, oddly enough, without knowing the other two or leaving it up to his wife to invite Frau von Liebenwein. He said it would give them the opportunity to meet charming members of Roman society. The count thanked him, promising that they would attend. Then they chatted about other things for a while. Des Essarts sat there, and his face really did look absentminded. He smoked one cigarette after another and, having removed his gloves, he waved them at the bees that buzzed around the honey. Then he told an anecdote that threatened to become a shaggy-dog story, and eventually fizzled out entirely. At last, he abruptly said goodbye.

"The following," said Maltravers when Des Essarts was gone, "likewise has no point: we will leave our cards with him and," he turned to Henrikstein, "send his wife flowers, which I must ask you to purchase. But still and all, I am curious how *this* story *really* ends."

ELEVEN

At the Des Essarts home, the Maltravers trio created a sensation, especially Henrikstein and Frau von Liebenwein, both of whom looked dazzling. After they had dressed, Maltravers had gazed at himself and the other two in the mirror and, shaking his head, he had stated that the way the three of them stood there, no one could possibly believe that they had nothing up their sleeve. I do, he murmured, have *something* up my sleeve. The Des Essartses lived on the first story of a mansion on Piazza di Spagna, facing the hill of the Pincio. Even the entranceway and the staircase, hazily illuminated by six-paned gold lanterns (stern lanterns of Baroque warships), but especially the salons in the light of multi-armed lusters with flickering glass tassels, showed fading and slightly peeling frescoes. In these paintings, so many unbelievably fleshy gods and other mythological figures wallowed and twisted about so curvaceously that compared with them, the living spectators in their evening garb at first looked almost consumptive—except, of course, Mme. des Essarts, who, in her state of decolleté and overlifesized muscularity, seemed like an enormous goddess who had stepped down from one of those Baroque frescoes. Next to her, Monsieur des Essarts cut an even tinier figure. Married couples, Maltravers instantly said to himself, who are physically so disharmonious have nearly always gotten together for more cogent reasons than harmony, usually business; for one almost never quite knows what such bizarre people live on; but if one does not know, then such people normally live very well, at least better than those about whom one does know what they live on. The latter, you see, almost never know how to live.

The count had further opportunities to admire the skill with which everything was managed here, starting with a knack for gathering guests with such great names, to a flair for locating a rental apartment with a framework like a palace. For people like the Des Essarts refused to commit themselves to any property of their own. They only rented. And even the decaying frescoes might have a secondary meaning; to permit a certain aristocratic neglect in other aspects of style. At least, the frescoes saved them the trouble of procuring tapestries. If you wish to live cheaply, then you should live grandly. For grandeur can never be fully maintained anyhow. In short, Mme. and Monsieur des Essarts proved extremely skillful in every respect. Even the most exclusive people instantly had a marvelous time here. Instead of being bored as a whole, the gathering automatically broke up into groups, in which the guests had wonderful conversations.

The Maltravers trio, after being presented all around, was soon facing the people with whom they were to spend the rest of the evening. Normally one gets into a conversation with the last person one meets, and the Maltravers trio began to converse with the small group of people with whom they wound up standing. These people were the following: a Count Montalto, a Signorina di Soria, and her fiancé, a Baron Spadaro.

"We've already met," Montalto said to Maltravers. But he too called him Fortescue. So their acquaintanceship could only be a very recent one.

"Yes," replied Maltravers, "indeed we have. In Milan."

Evidently Montalto was the person whom Maltravers had visited there.

However, he knew none of the other guests.

You see, the Des Essarts had shown him the guest list way in advance.

Pointing to two or three names, he had asked them not to invite those people—and Des Essarts, peculiarly enough, had actually crossed them off.

Otherwise nothing would have been easier here, in high society, than for Maltravers to bump into people he had known in the past. He had run the same risk in Paris, of course. But there too, before socializing, Maltravers had always asked to see the guest list, a wish that people had, for a short time, evidently put up with as an aristocratic spleen.

And if he was, nevertheless, recognized in a city, then the city was simply lost for him. After all, there were so many other cities in which he could play the man of honor: Madrid, Barcelona, Cairo, Berlin, London— which was so huge that one could be both a man of honor and not—New York—which was equally huge— Chicago, Valparaiso. . . . Still and all, he told himself, it would have been more convenient to have a spotless, or at least a lesser-known past. For actually he hated all those cities in which he had knocked about or would have to keep on knocking about. In moments of honesty with himself, he admitted that he had only talked himself into having to travel, at least during his first life. He would have much preferred remaining on an estate in Bohemia or Carinthia and from time to time going no further than to a neighboring nest to shop or to sell his harvest. And he would have read a lot and dreamt a lot. . . . For the grand world of high society is very little, and only the little world is big. A pond with whispering reeds in your homeland is worth more than the Étoile in Paris, and a forest nook is worth more than the entire Riviera. . . . It would have been very easy for him to begin a new life. But everyone else was still living the old life. That was it. A life is a whole world, but the world does not start a new life. An old life is stale and distasteful, but a new life always has something hurried about it. What is past is past—but not for others. Everyone who truly lives forgets. But the others do not really live. They merely keep remembering.

However, what Maltravers feared most was his renown as a dead man. No longer being alive had been so relaxing, so noncommittal. Gazing pensively at Montalto, Maltravers decided to socialize very little, at least here, not just for his own sake, but also because of Frau von Liebenwein. He had shown her the list, too, but he did not quite trust her memory for names. Nonetheless, she had not been recognized by anyone either.

"Apropos," Montalto turned to the count again, "are you related to the Fortescue-Maltraverses? I meant to ask you that in Milan."

When one sups with other counts, thought the count, one must obviously use a long spoon. However, he said no, he was not related to the Maltraverses.

"Then I congratulate you," said Montalto.

142

"Why?" asked Maltravers. "If I were, I could, I believe, even boast of being descended from kings."

"Ah," replied Montalto, "from what I have heard, there is no beggar in whom a drop of royal blood does not flow, and no king in whom a drop of beggar's blood does not flow. I, for example, do not set much store by the assumption that my family goes back to the Vandal kings, just as you would not have to be proud if you were a Maltravers. In that case, you would have a huge skeleton in your family closet."

"What kind of skeleton?" asked Maltravers.

And Montalto began to tell him Maltravers's life story up to his death. The others listened attentively. Frau von Liebenwein would have much preferred grinning from ear to ear, but she merely raised her eyebrows like a duchess who has learned that her chambermaid has forgotten herself with a lover, and Maltravers listened with only half an ear. He was bored at having to hear the story of his earlier life, it had become infinitely repulsive for him just to think of that life, and he listened only because he was waiting for the moment when Montalto would at last directly allude to his, Maltravers's, being Maltravers. But Montalto did not do so, at least not blatantly. Frau von Liebenwein, no doubt, thoroughly relished the scene. But Maltravers did not look at her. While he lay in wait for Montalto and perhaps Montalto for him, Maltravers gazed at the young people.

Rumor had it that even though Alba Soria was engaged to Spadaro, Montalto was interested in her. At least, that was what Des Essarts claimed. However, she apparently did not requite this interest. Nor did Henrikstein, as the count noticed, make any special impression on her. Evidently, she truly loved Spadaro, and Spadaro loved her too. She could not have really been called pretty. But she exuded a great deal of charm. People were probably enchanted by her expression of utter purity. She had something like an aura of hovering clarity. Leaving her convent at the age of nineteen, she had gotten engaged to Spadaro soon after. Spadaro was a Sicilian Norman, tall, bony, flaxen-haired— all in all, by no means particularly attractive. As a royal palace officer, he had little or no private means. But Alba could expect quite a sizable fortune. Nevertheless, she had decided in his favor without hesitating, not because she had liked him all that much, but because she had noticed how deeply he loved her; and she considered nothing less than her entire future life valuable enough to thank him with. It would have struck her as petty and unworthy to wait for others or to choose anyone else. But perhaps, thought Maltravers, gazing at Spadaro pensively, he is unworthy of her all the same. If couples meet, it is by sheer chance; if they fall in love, it is due to mere opportunity; and if they never fall out of love, then it is nothing but habit. It would ultimately be absurd not to acknowledge any other possibilities. For that would mean turning chance into providence. But women do not see such niceties; they simply accept everything. All men love all women at once, and all women love only the man they love. All women are only one woman to a man, and one man is all men to a woman.

Meanwhile, Montalto was telling about Maltravers's death. He apparently knew nothing about his resurrection, but eventually he indulged in numerous remarks of a general nature. He said that the whole cardsharp affair of the allegedly so great adventurer had been characteristic of the expected final collapse of an utterly mediocre mind. Maltravers calmly replied that failing to understand a collapse was, on the contrary, merely characteristic of a mediocre faculty of judgment. A man should be judged not by the ease of his successes, but by the greatness of his defeats. For a victory was due chiefly to the adversary's faults, while every defeat was due to one's own faults, and its greatness actually first proved the scope of a personality. And above all: only the man who has climbed very high can fall very low. Did he not agree, Maltravers asked Des Essarts.

But Des Essarts professed flight of ideas—he seemed quite unable to recall anything similar in his own life—and the practical Mme. des Essarts, bored by such unpractical discussions, showed the group her Herculean back—in which a curvaceous crease divided the tremendous musculature—and she joined the other guests. The flood of her golden hair flickered in the light of the lamps.

Montalto gazed after her for an instant, shrugged, and finally said to the count: "Do not judge Maltravers in those terms! His defeat had neither greatness nor depth. His was a very shallow fall. He went to prison, then he died. That is all."

"There is," said Maltravers, "no greater defeat than death. Death has every depth. But how would you know!"

"Do *you* know?" asked Montalto.

At that moment, a man with white hair and a dark moustache came in through the door from the other salon, glanced about, then walked over and put his arm around Alba's shoulder. "Well?" he said.

"Have you," the girl asked Frau von Liebenwein, "met my father?"

"Yes," said Maltravers, "we had the honor a bit earlier."

"And what," asked Soria, whose arrival had occasioned a pause, "were you talking about?"

"We were talking about death," said the young girl. "We often talked about it at the convent. However, Count Fortescue has very different views on these matters."

"In any case," said Soria, smiling, "it is so kind of you, count, to entertain my daughter that I dare not even find your topics bizarre. I am fully aware of my responsibility in bringing an engaged couple here. Such couples are usually so exclusively dependent on one another that they far too often only disturb the mood of a social gathering. It was all the friendlier of you to divert the two of them." And, with one arm around his daughter's shoulder, he patted Spadaro on the back with his other hand.

"You are being unfair to these young people," said Maltravers. "And even if an engaged couple are boring, they are then usually all the more amusing as a married couple. Apropos, it was not I who carried the conversation, but Count Montalto."

"Or perhaps," said Montalto, "it was really you, after all."

"Whatever you think," said Maltravers, shrugging. The hint was now clear enough. Montalto seemed downright afraid that the count had not quite caught his drift. The two men locked eyes, and another pause ensued. Frau von Liebenwein once again concealed a grin. Henrikstein held his tongue, since the conversation had taken place in Italian, which he did not understand.

"Apropos," Soria finally said, "if you people have nothing better to talk about than death, I personally do not believe in the significance of the so-called first death. The real death is the second death—" But he was interrupted, for Montalto suddenly guffawed.

146

"What's wrong?" asked Soria, astonished. "What's the matter?"

"I," laughed Montalto, pretending to wipe a tear from his eye, "I fully agree that the first death is not always very relevant! One can even survive it quite nicely, as it sometimes happens. But what do *you* mean?"

"Why, I don't know," said Soria, a bit rattled, "in what terms you were discussing the subject. I—"

"Well," Montalto egged him on, "just tell us!"

"I only meant," said Soria, "that the Book of Revelations already speaks of a twofold death, a physical one and a spiritual one."

"Well then," said Montalto. "You may not know," and he turned to Maltravers, "that Signor di Soria occasionally indulges in playing the prophet. In his leisure hours, he busies himself with reading the Apocalypse a bit, and he always suspects that the end of the world is nigh. So may I apologize for laughing."

"Apologize to Signor di Soria," said Maltravers, and, turning to the latter, he added: "I think you can put your mind at ease. There probably is no end of the world. There are only worlds. When one world perishes, the other ascends. Nor does the Evangelist mean anything else. After all, he himself already speaks about the new world."

"Yes," said Soria, "but that will not be ours anymore."

"The world is never ours anymore; it is always the world of the future. But what prompts you to have such peculiar ideas? Are you really studying such things?"

"Count Montalto," said Soria, "is exaggerating, of course. Nevertheless, such trains of thought should not surprise you here, in our country. We are accustomed to the sight of ruins. Here, in our country, a

147

world once really existed and perished. And conditions at the time of the fall of Rome are identical with, or at least very similar to, conditions today, when Europe is growing weary and her head is drooping on her shoulder. Why, then, should not our own end be nigh! Frankly, today our will to live is purely a will to exist. We have lived through too much to really want to go on living. We fear the future instead of hoping for it. We try to save what we still possess, and we squander what we have saved, for fear of losing it after all. Nor do we have any heirs. We are probably closer to the real end than the Empire was. I am not saying that the stars will fall from the sky and that the world will be consumed by fire or sink into the ocean. It will not go under. But it will become bleak and desolate. Mankind will die, the forest will grow across the lands again, and the seas will be empty."

"Yes," said Maltravers, "if death comes, then the forest will return; people often imagine that this will be the end. But I do not believe in an end. Nothing ends, everything goes on. And whatever goes under, goes under only in order to rise again. Is that not so, count Montalto? In short, I am not worried about the world. I have lived through too many worlds. I do not even think that Rome perished. I find that it still exists. I actually feel fine here, and I do not fear its end. The only thing I fear is that we are boring the others here with our discussion. But it would, of course, be a delight for me to continue my conversation with you, Signor di Soria. Come along! Let us go and drink a few glasses of champagne and leave the youngsters to their own devices. They will fare best that way."

And nodding to the others, he took Soria by the arm, and they went into the adjacent salon.

Maltravers then stayed on until two in the morning.

He had a fine conversation with Soria, or at least acted as if he were having a fine conversation with him. Soria, in any case, soon found him enchanting. He asked Maltravers to call on him. Soria lived on Via Quattro Fontane. He was said to be still extremely wealthy. However, the nobility of the —originally Spanish—family was dubious. It had made its way up by means of industries. Soria himself was scarcely active now. Following the death of his second wife, he had placed Alba in a convent and then done some traveling. Now that Alba was living with him again, he resided partly in Rome and partly at his country estate Torre de' Conti. He read a great deal and consequently had rather crotchety opinions, but his crotchetiness was one of those charming eccentricities to be found among the rich or among members of old families. For a family can age even if it is still relatively young. He was absorbed chiefly in the Apocalypse. He projected his own gentle decay into the world and was distinctly comforted by the thought that nothing much would go on after him. The dreadful fantasies of Revelations, the grand blasting of horns, the demise of cities, and the collapse of the heavens gave him an extremely pleasant satisfaction. The conviction that the world might nevertheless go on would have made him nervous. But his mind was put at ease by the announced end.

Naturally, he discussed other things with Maltravers, and they rambled from one subject to the next. Meanwhile, Henrikstein conversed in French with Alba and Spadaro, while Frau von Liebenwein had a long talk with Mme. des Essarts. For even though one woman was a sort of domestic and the other a sort of aristocrat, they got along famously. While not discussing anything crucial, they nevertheless felt that if they *had* discussed anything crucial, they would instantly have been of one mind. But Mme. des Essarts merely railed against the servants, and Frau von Liebenwein railed against the aristocrats, each woman agreeing with the other; and when the guests finally departed, the consensus was that the evening had been a complete success.

TWELVE

In late March, Lolita arrived in Rome. She had been hired at the Arizona, starting in April. Henrikstein had found her the job behind Maltravers's back. She arrived at nine A.M. on the same train that had brought Maltravers and Henrikstein and then Frau von Liebenwein. Everyone coming from the north arrives in Rome at nine A.M. Travelers likewise reach Berlin in the morning, Paris at noon, and Vienna and London in the evening. Every city has its time of arrival. Some people, of course, do arrive at other times, but then they do not fit properly into the cities to which they travel.

Henrikstein and Lola had corresponded. But their letters had always been short, vague, and slightly awkward, full of the usual formulas and howlers they had learned while writing letters in their childhood. When Lola got off the train, they went toward one another and kissed, not in their usual way, but, since they were at a railroad station, in the somewhat conventional and clumsy way in which simple people kiss at railroad stations. And after kissing, they both spoke at the same time, so that they did not understand one another. Then they left. But as they left, he had recovered the gait and lightness of an athlete and she the gait of a dancer.

Henrikstein carried Lola's baggage. It had not crossed his mind that it could be carried by another person. Whenever he had picked up someone at a station, he had carried the baggage. Outside the terminal, they hailed a cab. Henrikstein indicated the address: Via del Babuino. It was not far from where the Des Essarts lived.

Inside the car, he held Lola's hands in his. They could have kissed again, but they did not; they had never kissed anyone in a cab after calling for him at the station. Indeed, they had never taken a car, they had always ridden the trolley. At first, they were silent; then they began to speak. But they asked each other very trivial things: what the weather had been like in Paris, and what it was like in Rome, and how they were in general, and how had Lola's trip been. Good, said Lola. Henrikstein said that he was quite well too. Then he squeezed her hands and, after a time, wondered whether he should let them go, but he continued clutching them.

He had rented a room for Lola on the third landing of a house on Via del Babuino. He carried her baggage up the stairs, the landlady came out and spoke Italian to Lola. Meanwhile, Henrikstein brought the baggage into the room, and Lola followed him. Inside, there were two bouquets on the table.

"What lovely flowers!" said Lola. "From you?"

"Yes," said Henrikstein. "The red ones. The others are probably from the landlady."

Lola picked up the red bouquet and pressed her face

152

into the flowers; then she put them back on the table, turned around, and kissed Henrikstein, and he kissed her, for after all, once you came home, it was all right to kiss again.

"Do you like the room?" he asked.

"Yes," she said, "very much"; and she looked around.

But now they would have to unpack, he finally said. So they unpacked Lola's bags, and as they hung the dresses in the closet, he said that a few hangers were missing. When the landlady was summoned, she said she had only the hangers that were there; so Henrikstein said he would buy a few. While Lola washed her face and hands, he sat on the bed. Lola smelled the flowers once again, then they went down for breakfast.

They had breakfast in a small caffè with open windows. Trucks and autos drove past, and carts that had brought produce to the city lumbered by with particolored wheels. Laundry was hung out to dry from the windows of the opposite houses. The pure air wafting from the sea was already mingling with the smell of cooking oil, and the odor of benzene hovered in the air. A swarm of pink-footed pigeons whirled by in a flutter and alighted on the street; they were frightened away, then they perched on the cornices of buildings, but soon returned to the street. Somewhere a child shouted, and one could see the gesticulations and hear the suddenly disrupted conversations of people passing the windows of the caffè.

Henrikstein said he was happy that Lola was here, but he asked her whether she wanted to go upstairs and take a nap. No, she said, she didn't have time; she had to go to the Arizona and announce her arrival. Yes, said Henrikstein, she had to do that. So he said he would accompany her there and then return to the hotel. But they wanted to meet again after dinner. Or

153

did Lola want to go to sleep after dinner? No, she said, she had slept enough on the train, and she would rather go strolling with Henrikstein. Where could they go here? Maybe, said Henrikstein, he would be able to call for her in Maltravers's automobile. Yes, said Lola, that would be lovely.

So he paid, and they left. He escorted her to the Arizona, then returned to the hotel. After dinner, he fetched her in the automobile.

They drove to Tivoli and sat down at one of the tables. First they gazed at the landscape, where the shadows of clouds flew over the hilly waves like the shadows of gigantic schooners. Then, for the first time, they began to discuss their plans. They did have plans now. They were engaged, after all. They wanted to get married.

Henrikstein said he had begun training again. He was working out with Gauntlett every morning. He had also tried to find a manager, he said, but hadn't yet been able to get anyone interested. After the misfortune he had suffered in Paris two years ago, he was still considered a has-been, even here in Rome. Nevertheless, he felt he could attempt a real fight again. Maybe not right away. But at least in the very near future. As he talked about his condition, Lola listened with the face of a simple person who thinks he knows that a misfortune is not a personality defect, but can happen to anyone. Henrikstein said that Maltravers was actually against his training. He had said he had other plans for Henrikstein. What sort of plans? asked Lola. Henrikstein said he didn't know, but maybe Maltravers meant a rich wife.

Lola kept silent for a moment, then, lowering her eyes, she asked why Henrikstein didn't actually want a rich wife.

Because he loved Lola, said Henrikstein.

She looked at him and gave him her hand to kiss, with the slightly studied motion that she had learned in nightclubs when men told her she was pretty and she believed she had to act like a lady. But she meant it very sincerely. Henrikstein kissed her hand, then said: Just a couple of months ago, he may have dreamt of marrying a rich woman. But now he hoped he wouldn't have to at all. He would manage to earn some money himself and marry Lola. He didn't believe he would be allowed to box right away. He would probably have to reenter the ring as a sparring partner, but he hoped to excel in this and catch the eye of some manager. Maltravers must have been right when he had said that he, Henrikstein, needed diversion and relaxation more than anything else. He really felt totally fit, especially since he had resumed training; after first losing some weight, he had started gaining again, his reach was wider than before, and his breathing was very good. He was only surprised that Maltravers, as he had said, was not interested in any of this, and that he must have completely changed his mind.

That, said Lola with a shrug, might be so. What had the two of them, he and the count, been doing here— whom had they been seeing, and so on.

Mainly, said Henrikstein, the Sorias. And he told her about the Sorias, and that they had often gone out together, or taken drives in Soria's or Maltravers's automobile, once even all the way to Naples, and also to Lake Albano and to Lake Nemi to look at the ancient ship that had been in the water and had been taken out, and he would accompany Alba when she went shopping downtown in the mornings. But Alba was engaged, and he had also told her that he too was engaged, and she had been very glad and had congratulated him. Lola blushed slightly. In any case, Henrikstein went on, Maltravers had never directly told him what to do or expressly wished something or made any other suggestion. He had only stated what he did not wish: namely, Henrikstein's return to boxing.

That, Lola finally said, was really odd. She asked Henrikstein various questions about the count, his habits and moods, and the two of them made all sorts of guesses about him, but got nowhere, and then gave up fairly soon, for they were not used to racking their brains about the tastes of people, some of whom enjoyed sitting with girls in nightclubs, and others who were intent on watching pugilists smashing one another's heads in. These two young people had been too dependent on their professions to love them or even be interested in them, and they also viewed the boxer's strange relationship to Maltravers as a secondary aspect of Henrikstein's work. Granted, both he and Lola had originally loved their professions and been interested in them. However, it soon turned out that they were not really practicing their callings. Lola's dancing did not, to state it precisely, interest anyone. Evening after evening, men with bellies and bald heads sat in the nightclub, or men without bellies or bald heads, fat ones and skinny ones, repulsive ones and slightly less repulsive ones, and none of them really cared whether her dancing was good or not. They all merely ogled her legs and her figure and the way she moved, and they judged the girls solely by whether or not they wished to drink with the customers afterwards. And finally, the girls judged themselves by that standard. They were like merchandise. And Henrikstein too had been merchandise, with which the managers could make money or not; and once he had ruined himself by making money for them, no one had made any money off him anymore. So he had become worthless, just as Lola was sure to be worthless in ten years, when no one would be interested in her legs anymore. For there was no singer now to celebrate the boxing matches and no Hellenes to watch the procession of virgins at the panathenaea; there were only salesmen who had left their wives at home and gone traveling to foreign cities, where they gawked at the dancing girls of today. Now, there was no world behind Henrikstein's fists or Lola's dance-steps, their work had no meaning anymore. Every new generation was ready, always ready, to perform new labor for the world; but the world no longer existed, or what was still known as the world sold off its labor from wheeler to dealer, making it meaningless.

Thus, Henrikstein was actually not even grateful to the count for enabling him to lead such a life. He felt that he was quite simply being paid not to box now, just as earlier he had been paid to box. Besides, simple people are really quite indifferent to the kind of work they obtain. They want to work in order to live, but they are also willing to be paid for not working. They seldom criticize employers as long as there is work. They may notice awkward things, but they put up with incomprehensible things, yet never view their employers as crazy. Workers have too many problems of their own to worry about other people's problems. This is true of anyone who really has to work. In any case, Lola would certainly have preferred never again to put on dancing shoes and Henrikstein never again to put on six-ounce gloves if events had taken a different turn. But she had to go to the Arizona, and he had to think about a comeback. For both of them the fault lay with

157

the taste of a class of people whom they did not understand, and the man they understood least of all was Maltravers.

They sat there for a while, Lola smoking a cigarette, Henrikstein not smoking. Finally, they stood up and went to do some motoring around the Sabine Mountains. The air was as clear as glass, and the moon was like a small, rosy cloud in the afternoon sky. At the place where bushes dangled over the narrow road, they stopped, and hugged and kissed ardently, on and on. But eventually, somewhat embarrassed, they leaned back in their seats because they suddenly felt like people who have nothing more sensible in mind.

Toward six, they drove back to the city.

THIRTEEN

April was fairly warm, May soon grew extremely hot. From the hills, the fragrance of flowers wafted down to Rome in clouds, blending with the bitter scent of heated laurel, and the wind from the countryside bore the smell of hay through the marble streets and to the glowing squares. The city was thoroughly transformed; it became more exotic, more sacred, and more sinister. Some gods or other, who had been driven away for the winter like migratory birds, must have come back and were nesting on the consecrated heights. Or at least that was claimed by Maltravers, who had brought up this theory. Tremendous showers of light fell from the sky, and, from behind the cliffside castles and the ridges of hills, dusty golden clouds rose like giant towers into the flickering radiance.

When Henrikstein was training, the sweat poured down his back, and Gauntlett could no longer endure the climate. He sweated, cursed, and swore he would return to England immediately. During the past few

days, he brought over various Italians, whom Henrikstein beat up with remarkable style. He had achieved
an unusually good form. Of course, no manager could
have been found to get him a fight. But he was hired as
one of the sparring partners for Jack Joyce, who was
scheduled to fight Gonella in early June.

Henrikstein pinned all his hopes on the demonstration bout with Joyce.

If Lola had not had to stay up too late the previous
evening, she would sometimes drop by when he was
training. And one morning (Lola was not there), who
should show up but Maltravers. After a moment of
wavering, Henrikstein wanted to stop the fight and
greet him, but Maltravers shook his head; he sat down
on a chair and watched him pensively for a time.

"And the hair on his head," the count murmured to
himself, "began to grow back where it had been shorn."
It was a passage about Samson in the Book of Judges.
Once, in order to obtain a divorce, Maltravers had become Protestant for a while, taking the opportunity to
read the Bible. Since then, God had disintegrated for
him into a plethora of gods. He lit a cigarette, crossed
his legs, and gazed up at Henrikstein. The boy's musculature played along his arms and over his naked back as
if mice were scurrying under the skin, which was like
silk, and the floor of the ring boomed softly under the
elastic movements of the heavyweight. His strength
was restored like that of Samson. The hero had to toil
in the mill for the Philistines, who had shorn off his
hair, the source of his divine strength; but his hair
began to grow back. All strength ultimately comes
from God or from the gods. Even the strongest man
loses all his strength if the gods turn away from him.
The boy's locks had been shorn like those of a slave by
the wheeler-dealers: the managers, the racketeers, the

160

traffickers in human flesh, the poverty, the lower depths of life. But Maltravers had started that hair growing again. It now grew like the hair of a freeman.

The hair was dark blond, almost brunette, like the eyebrows, but with a touch of gold, as if strewn with gold dust; one would have thought that bits of the gold dust would have to keep falling to the shoulders and remain there. The count looked at that hair and thought of his own. . . . But finally, he left without so much as indicating what he thought of the training. Nor did he talk about it later; for that was just his way of being neither for nor against something, even if he personally wished one thing or the other. Granted, he had objected to Henrikstein's idea of returning to the ring. But that was weeks ago. Meanwhile, the count had changed. Gazing at the door that Maltravers had closed behind him, Henrikstein suddenly realized how greatly the count had changed. He may have changed earlier. But in Paris, Henrikstein hadn't noticed. Here in Rome, the change had become very profound. Nevertheless, Henrikstein would have been unable to put his finger on it. Maltravers was still the same and yet also someone else. Earlier, for example, he had spoken disparagingly about many things. Now, he occasionally still talked a great deal, but no longer condemned anything. He would put up with even the most contradictory things as though he had realized that everything is completely different from what can be said about it, and yet completely the same. And if Henrikstein had never known what Maltravers was planning or what he was actually involved in, he now at least knew for certain that the count did absolutely nothing. It had always been an axiom of the count's not to want things to happen, but to let them occur on their own. For, he said, one can interfere with events, but never

161

truly determine them. Now he no longer seemed to have any intention whatsoever of interfering with anything. He let everything run its course. So Henrikstein could have disregarded the count. Indeed, he *was* disregarding him, yet he had the uncanny feeling that he was merely going along with the count's wishes; and sometimes, he felt that Maltravers's wishes had nothing to do with whatever was happening, as if someone else were behind it, as if Merlin had cast a spell on everything, or as if the count himself were serving an intention or a providence that was being realized of its accord.

In any case, Maltravers seemed so thoroughly free of any need ever to make his own decisions again that he devoted himself entirely to his peculiar brand of contemplation and made no personal dispositions, but did only what others proposed. He received many invitations and accepted each and every one, utterly unconcerned whether somebody might or might not recognize him or Frau von Liebenwein. He used his car a great deal, either taking the wheel or having Henrikstein drive him; he spent several days in Naples and Capri and, above all, frequently visited the Sorias at Torre de' Conti. He conversed with Signor di Soria for hours on end, while reclining in a deck chair in the shade of the house, drinking orangeade, gazing at the silver green waves of the unmown grass and the rustling foliage clouds of the trees, and arguing against the end of the world. He had of late been unusually attentive to his wardrobe, and his motions were spare, as if he were always concentrating only on keeping his appearance from becoming disorderly. And while he spoke, lying in the deck chair, he either picked motes of dust from his suit or broodingly pointed his cane at things that had no connection whatsoever to what he was saying.

"The world," he said, aiming his cane like a pistol, first at the tips of his own summer shoes, then at Soria's aperitif, "the world is not the globe, the light, the sky, the rivers, the thunder, and the stars; nor the masses of people thronging the cities, nor the wildlife, the herds, and the swarms of fish in the ocean; nor does Atlas carry the world on his shoulders. Rather, everyone carries it inside his own head. For the world is only exactly as much life as a person lives himself. When I sleep, the world stands still, and when I am dead, it no longer exists. A star that I do not see does not shine in the sky, and a woman whom I do not know has not yet lived. But when I live, everything exists: all stars and all women. And the world no more goes under than it comes up like the sun. Yet it takes only one glance to make the world exist; a flutter of the eyelashes, and the world is gone; another glance, and it is back. For the world is more than the sun. The world itself is the eye to which it reveals itself, the ear in which it sounds, the fingers that feel it. Feeling, they say, is everything. The world is a feeling of the world, that is all. If I do not feel, then the world does not exist. There is no other end of the world. And did not God himself indulge in proving that his world is practically nothing, and man everything! Did he not, from time to time, hand over the dominion of the globe to someone, so that this ruler would pass it on immediately: Constantine or that Charles from the House of Hapsburg! The kingdoms, the armies and navies, Byzantium and Rome, the Holy Empire, Flanders and Kyburg and Cleves, Castille, Leon and Aragon, Granada and the islands of the ocean, both Sicilies and both Indies—did the emperor not give them away just as a man discards things that are nothing but trouble, and did he not shed his dignities like a bothersome robe! For a real apple, in the hand of a child, is more of an apple than the imperial pome, which merely *signifies* the world, in an emperor's hand!"

FOURTEEN

On May twenty-ninth, Soria gave a party at Torre de'
Conti: Alba was to be presented to the queen on the
thirtieth. They therefore decided not to let the party
stretch out far beyond midnight. For the Sorias wanted
to get back to town that night. Nevertheless, Henrikstein was rather unhappy about the invitation, since he
was scheduled to fight Jack Joyce the next day. Being
in form was all that mattered to him. He should have
gone to bed early and neither smoked nor drunk, but
he did not dare say a word to Maltravers. He therefore
made up his mind at least not to touch a cigarette and
to let the alcohol simply stand during the dinner.

He drove the count and Frau von Liebenwein out to
Torre de' Conti. They left Rome around six o'clock. A
storm was brewing in the heavens.

A strong wind fragrant with rain soon blasted
against the car, and looking back, they saw that the city,
even way above the church domes and hilltops, was already swathed in tremendous veils of haze and clouds

of yellow and silvery blue marble dust, which blended with the vapors of the sky.

In the mountains, the thunder rolled as if horses were making a racket in wooden stalls, and the world was almost pitch-dark. But toward the south west, one last patch of sky shone enamel blue through the dust wafting over the city. All at once, from both sides of the asphalt road, tiny white cloudlets flew up like gunshots; the storm plunged down in its full fury, pummeling the car as if with fists. The car slowed down perceptibly, and a wall of rain, shining ghostlike, and soon turning into hail, roared and rattled past. The hail drummed on the roof of the car, splattering everywhere like splintering glass. Frau von Liebenwein, who was dreadfully afraid, began murmuring a few Lord's Prayers and Hail Marys, as she had always done during storms in her youth, with the other servants in the kitchen. But at every crack of lightning, which glowed sulphurous through the strands of ice, she lost all control and cursed so fiercely that it was a delight to hear. Maltravers, leaning back in the seat next to her, listened respectfully to her prayers and amusedly to her curses.

The torrent of hail lasted several minutes, then turned back into rain; roughly half an hour later, the rain stopped altogether, and the storm rolled away like artillery booming across the sea. By the time they pulled up at Torre de' Conti, with a long, drawn-out signal as if a dwarf were blowing an ivory horn, the final vapors were vanishing from the twilit sky, whose color was already passing into the lavender blue of the night. Now, the fog spun knee-deep only on the meadows.

Torre de' Conti, the "Tower of the Counts," was an enormous villa that had been built by a Cardinal Orsini

166

on the site of a demolished papal castle. The Sorias had already owned it for some sixty years. It stood at the foot of the mountains; and the gardens, descending in terraces full of laurel and roses, stretched all the way down into the flatlands.

A large company had gathered. The Trasmondis were here, relatives of Soria's first wife; and Enzio Foschi, Alba's cousin, with young Signora Grimaldi from Venice, whom he loved, and her husband, with whom he, consequently, got along far, far better than with her; Baron Spadaro; the old Duke di Gravina; Des Essarts with his herculean spouse; a Livonian Baron Fredericks; the beautiful Julia Porcaro; the Rumanian envoy, Gaetano Oderisi, Count di Traetto; seven or eight Savellis (for this family was already so huge that it was no longer a family, but an epidemic); Arlotto Frajapane with his titian-haired wife, Anna Visconti, who was crossed-eyed like an otter; Lord and Lady Stutfield; the blonde Lady Barbara Modish, who had once been a model; the Raineriis; Count Montalto; two Tornabuonis; the Marquis de Lenoncourt; a certain Herr von Kussmaul; several dreadfully tall and skinny American women; an unknown female with a floury complexion and amazingly huge emeralds; the two old Parentucellis; the Guidobaldis; the Perottis; and many others.

The soirée was meant to sort of precelebrate Alba's presentation at court. The young girl was repeatedly toasted, and she was very happy. For she was to marry in two weeks.

After dinner, they danced. Frau von Liebenwein had another excellent conversation with Mme. des Essarts, who railed against the heat in Rome, and Frau von Liebenwein railed against the storm. Soria gazed at the dancers with a worried mien, as if this party were evoking the end of the world; but Maltravers managed to dissuade him.

"Put your mind at ease, dear friend," he said. "These families, who survived the machinations of the Borgias, will most likely survive an evening at the Sorias. For man is astoundingly flexible. If these people, the grandchildren of condottieres, Renaissance natures, renowned district captains and poisoners—if they were spirited to some other place in their tuxedoes and evening gowns, they could just as easily make up a company of harmless businessmen in a hotel vestibule at Carlsbad or Marienbad. . . . For human beings do not die out, they merely change. Even the most ancient families still exist, officially or unofficially. Indeed, the more banal they become, the more swiftly they multiply, sort of the way rabbits procreate more massively than lions. I am also convinced that, say, your domestics have just as good, or if you prefer, just as universal an ancestry as your guests. Montalto is right: There is really no beggar without royal blood, and no king without beggar's blood. My secretary, for example, is, as far as I know, the only person here who is not an aristocrat. He does not even have the financial, albeit, of course, still very minor, distinction of these American women, and yet he looks better than any of us, except perhaps Frau von Liebenwein. The truth of the matter is that the world, which you always believe to be so old, is incredibly young. The time when we were all actually related is still ludicrously recent. It was just a piddling four or five thousand years ago, no more than that. It need not have been earlier than the days when the first pharaohs were already radiant in the horizon of their palaces that the nations later known as Celts, Mycenians, Franks, Persians, Slavs, Greeks, Scythians, Nor-

168

mans, and Indians—that all these people nested together in the region of the Baltic or the Urals, looking alike and speaking the same language, a small tribe numbering several thousand souls. And then the Vedic knights set out for the Punjab, the Greeks for Morea, the Celts for France, the Romans for Etruria; and eventually more and more tribes migrated down from the north and subjugated the gruel of nations that had meanwhile formed here, around the Mediterranean. But in those days, people knew that all our kings, the Walsungens and the Gothic princes, the guardians of the Grail, Agamemnon's clan and the Julian imperial family, the Celtic chieftains and the rajahs were related closely enough, and the Aesir were related to the kings, and the kings to the people. Everyone could find his own forebears in the geneological tables of gods and men. By the way, do you know who the first gods were, Soria? Not the spirits of storms or fruitfulness, nor those of the sun or moon. The first gods were wild animals, from whom people fancied they had descended by eating them. Your god is what you eat. You can still see that every day at churches. . . . In short, the race of mortals is still too young to really die out, and the world is still too new to go under. We still live in a very early dawn, Soria. So do not flirt with the weariness of truly ancient races. When your ancestors were still dockworkers and fishwives, mine had stopped being kings long ago. And you can see: I still exist! Alas, alas!"

And he patted Soria, who was sharply affected by these liberties, on the shoulders, left him standing, and strolled back through the rooms. But the expression on his face indicated that he was still brooding about something. Finally, with his hands in his pockets, he stepped over to one of the large mirrors and looked at his reflection to check if any cigarette ashes had dropped on his tuxedo. But there were no ashes there. Nevertheless, he whisked some imaginary specks of dust from his lapels, adjusted the white flower in the buttonhole, and finally viewed his face in the mirror.

The hair on his head had grown back long ago; it was gray, but the eyebrows were still dark. His eyes, however, like the hair, had whitened—they were almost pale blue, like ice—and when he peered into his eyes, their reflections blurred into the floating light in the mirror and the mirrored room. A different world, a glittering world, was in the glass; the glass did not show the world as it was in reality. Perhaps, he thought, the mirrored world is more real than ours, for it could be that certain things reveal themselves only in the mirror but not in truth. In a mirror, one might, he thought, see things of which only the images exist, and not the realities. Then again, the mirror could also simply *not* show things. For some things may have no images. The mirror would just omit them. Conceivably, he thought, I could stand before the mirror and yet not be in the mirror. If I were dead, for example. Then the mirror could no longer show me. But I might then be able to step into the mirror and I would be in the mirror without standing before it. Now, however, I am still standing before the mirror and in the mirror at once. Thus, I am not dead. But, I could see other things in the mirror, things I usually do not see. Myself, primarily. After all, one never sees oneself. One sees the world, but one does not see oneself. Even the most invisible things are more visible than oneself. One is oneself the invisible. So it does not prevail from the outside, it prevails out of oneself. There is nothing that does not come from within oneself. Nothing, not even that which prevails, could come if I myself did not call to it and say: Come!

At that moment, he saw that Montalto was coming

toward him from the back, and he halted behind Maltravers.

Maltravers slowly turned around. Did I, he wondered, call him too? Yes, I called him too.

"Well?" asked Montalto after a moment.

"Well?" said Maltravers.

"You are gazing into the mirror," said Montalto, "in order to observe whether the things that you observe so little in reality are proceeding as desired."

"Frankly," replied Maltravers, "I seldom observe them anymore. After all, they proceed as desired anyhow."

"I do not think so."

"I *do*," said Maltravers, lighting a cigarette. "Everything is proceeding as desired."

"But not according to *my* desires."

"Or mine," said Maltravers. "But they are nevertheless proceeding as desired. Things simply proceed as they proceed. Neither your intentions nor mine make any difference."

"What do you mean?" asked Montalto, frowning.

"Exactly what I am saying," said Maltravers, blowing the smoke over Montalto's head. "What can happen happens. But it happens all on its own. Everything happens only on its own. I have come to realize that. I let things take their course. You should do the same. It makes no sense interfering with events. If one does interfere, one achieves only what one does not wish. You too would achieve nothing. Events can be influenced only if you yourself have nothing else in mind and are in a good mood. But you are not always in a good mood—for instance, now, and a certain bad mood has also taken hold of those involved. You, for instance, are already in a bad mood, and, frankly speaking, so am I. So let us not bore ourselves with our private little affairs. Have not you too grown weary of constantly making your own decisions? I grew weary of that long ago. Let us allow things to make their own decisions. They are stronger than we. They prevail on their own. That is known as: God's mills. God's mills, we are told, grind slowly. But sometimes they grind quickly. You shall see how quickly they will suddenly grind, Montalto!"

"Sir," Montalto snapped, "I am not interested in your general homilies. I was never interested in them. You've been in Rome for almost three months now, but you've done nothing. You have only accepted payment, that's all. You are a swindler! I knew you were, and I should have known better. You agreed to prevent this presentation to the queen. But you have not done so. Well, if you haven't done it, then I'll do it!"

"You?" Maltravers asked indifferently.

"Yes, I! And you can rest assured that you will again play the role that you did not care to play, Maltravers!"

Maltravers, his arm leaning on the mirror console, gazed at him for several moments. "Aha," he finally said. "Well, Montalto, you knew it from the very start. The first time we met at the Des Essarts home, you could not drop enough hints, even at the risk of jeopardizing our entire program. Since Gomez had not told you who I am, and since I did not tell you in Milan, did you have such a good time demonstrating to me that you know your Gotha? To what end? Perhaps to let me know that you had me in your hands? Yes? Well, no one has me in his hands anymore, Count Montalto. I was a prisoner long enough, and now I am not even my own prisoner. I do only as I wish. And you too, for all I care, may do as you wish." And he crushed his cigarette in an ashtray.

Montalto took a step toward him. "You would," he

said slowly, "really dare to risk it?"

"Yes," said Maltravers. "For I am risking nothing."

"Oh, but you are. You are risking everything, because you did not wish to do something that would have been a mere bagatelle for you. You have done things that were far worse. Why did you suddenly not wish to?"

"Because I do not like you," said Maltravers. "Like so many other people, you are considered correct because your actions do not go beyond the framework of the law. But the framework of the law is meaningless. As narrow as it sometimes is, it is also endlessly broad. The most probable things are prohibited, and the most improbable are permitted. No, Montalto, your correctness is not to your credit. You are unfair, Montalto. One is correct only in relation to other people, and fair chiefly to oneself. An action is worthy or worthless only if it has no judge. You are correct, but not fair. I was always incorrect, Montalto, but nevertheless I was always fair. I regret my cases of unfairness. I am delighted to note that my delays have frustrated your uncharming intentions. You still have the possibility, as you accurately remarked, to carry them out on your own. But you will only be endangering yourself. And above all, you will ultimately achieve nothing. So by all means, do it. Go ahead, Montalto, and do as you wish. You will achieve nothing but what will happen anyhow. I am ready for it, and frankly, I expect it and even desire it."

Montalto glared at him. "Go to the devil, Maltravers!" he finally hissed.

"I very well may do that," Maltravers laughed. "It will be a very nice confrontation between the two of us. Apparently, there is a good reason why this house is named Torre de' Conti. Well, in any case," and he motioned to him, "please leave me now. Hail and farewell!"

Montalto turned on his heel, cursing, and stalked out. Maltravers gazed after him. Then he straightened up, walked into the next room, and signaled to Frau von Liebenwein.

They waited until Henrikstein, who was dancing, bowed to his partner. Then Maltravers said to him: "Come on! We are leaving. You two need not make your goodbyes."

However, another group of guests was also leaving, and the Maltravers trio had to pass the Sorias, who were standing at the entrance, saying good night to the guests, who were stepping into their automobiles.

"I hope," Soria said to Maltravers, "that the three of you will afford us the pleasure of coming for tea tomorrow in Rome. By then, Alba will be able to tell you what it was like at the Quirinal."

"Do not forget," Maltravers, smiling oddly, told Henrikstein as they got into the car, "do not forget to be at Via Quattro Fontane tomorrow, at the very latest by five–thirty. Alba will give you a detailed account of everything that has happened in the meantime."

With that, the automobile took off. The Sorias, after saying good night to their final guests, likewise drove back to town. Montalto, in his heavy car, soon caught up with the others. That night, he wrote a long letter to the Comptroller of the Queen's Household. The letter was delivered by messenger at the crack of dawn.

On this thirtieth of May, several hundred young ladies of the aristocracy and society were to be presented to the queen. Long lines of traffic filled the streets around the palace, inching slowly toward the Quirinal. Most of the vehicles were automobiles, but now and then, in honor of the festive occasion, there were also two-horse and four-horse coaches, indeed, even a team of six cream-colored horses belonging to a Neapolitan banker with an ugly daughter. In her jewelry and white frock, she looked so sad and poignant among all the other, mostly pretty girls—so poignant that the young Prince di Colledimezzo, who, being penniless, was sharing a rental car with his sister and was stuck next to the coach-and-six for such a long time, fell in love with the banker's daughter and shortly thereafter married her, thus restoring the glory of his dynasty.

In general, during the often very lengthy pauses and tie-ups, there was a great deal of chatting between vehicles; indeed, some of the last arrivals, who assumed they would have to wait for hours on end, began playing bridge or piquet to while away the time. Thick crowds lined both sides of the motorcade, gaping at the clothes, the jewelry, and the vehicles. It was a beautiful day, less hot than the preceding ones; the wind wafted blossoms over the cars and the scent of many flowers that hung in waves over the garden's walls.

It took the Soria automobile from one to three P.M. to reach the square of the Quirinal. The catastrophe occurred at three.

As they turned into the piazza, Spadaro, in a gold-embroidered uniform, strode over to their car, and, greeting the Sorias, slowly walked alongside it. Alba wore a pale blue gown and had a bouquet of white roses in her lap. Her face was purer than alabaster. Spadaro gazed at her, he looked very happy, and he said he was convinced the queen would address especially distinguishing words to Alba. At that instant, a second palace officer strode up to the car, which had again come to a halt.

"Signor di Soria?" he asked.

Soria said, "Yes?" and the officer, leaning over to him in the car, whispered something into his ear.

Soria seemed not to understand him fully and gaped at him in amazement. "Excuse me?" he asked.

"You have been requested," the officer said in a restrained but very decisive tone, "not to present the young lady to Her Majesty."

Soria still did not understand, and Alba, under the broad rim of her white summer hat, turned a merely astounded face toward the officer. But all the blood drained from Spadaro's face, even his lips. "What," he stammered, "does this mean, Signor della Santa Croce? Which young lady should not be presented? Signorina di Soria?"

"Yes."

"Why?"

"Those are my orders."

"But why?"

"I am not empowered to tell you, Baron Spadaro. In any case, Signorina di Soria will not be received."

"Impossible!" Spadaro gasped. "There must be a mistake."

"I do not think so," said Santa Croce, glancing at Alba, then averting his eyes. "I have strict orders to ask Signor di Soria not to drive into the palace."

"From whom?" shouted Spadaro.

"I beg your pardon?"

"Who gave you these orders!?"

"The Comptroller of the Queen's Household."

Soria and Alba, both of them aghast, kept looking back and forth between the two men, and from the cars in front or behind, several heads turned around when Spadaro raised his voice.

"If the gentlemen would please care to speak more softly," said Soria finally, "and you, Signor della Santa

Croce, could you please explain to me more clearly what has happened. I absolutely do not comprehend you."

"Attempts were made," said Santa Croce, "to reach you, first by telephone, then through Signor di Papareschi, who was sent to your home to inform you personally. But he was unable to do so. Your party had already left. Consequently, I can only request here and now that you refrain from presenting Signorina di Soria to Her Majesty."

At that instant, the motorcade started moving again, made little headway, and soon halted.

"But why?" Soria cried to Santa Croce, who had been walking alongside with Spadaro and now stopped again by the car.

Santa Croce shrugged.

"I must ask you," cried Soria, "to tell me the reason, Signor della Santa Croce."

Once again, several heads turned, and Santa Croce said: "Do you really feel that this is the suitable place? Besides, you will soon be reaching the entrance to the Quirinal, and I must expressly beg you not to drive in. Please leave the line and drive home with your daughter, Signor di Soria! It is the only possibility."

Soria acted as if he were about to leap from the car and grab Santa Croce by the throat. But Alba, who had turned as white as the roses in her lap, clutched his arm. "Father," she said, "it must be a mistake, but let's go home all the same. It's better this way."

"Of course," cried Soria, "it can only be a mistake, but I cannot turn around!"

"Why not?"

"Under what pretext should I do so?"

"I don't know. But tell the chauffeur to drive home."

"Impossible!"

"People are staring at us!" cried Alba.

"Let them stare! We have to drive on. I cannot sit back and let you become an object of speculation for all of Rome tomorrow. Signor della Santa Croce! I have no idea what has happened, and I realize we do not have the time to investigate at this point. Naturally, I will forgo the presentation to the queen until the whole matter has been cleared up. But you cannot possibly demand that we do not drive in. You must let us drive in! You can then take us to a different exit, for all I care, and we can leave, but do not force us to get out of the line now, Signor della Santa Croce! Think of the scandal! Because of some mistake, which is certain to be cleared up, we will become the laughing stock of the city. Please let us drive up to the entrance, I implore you! Please do us at least this favor! And if you do not wish to do it for our sake, then please do it for Spadaro."

Santa Croce looked down at the ground, and Soria, clutching the edge of the car door, remained leaning forward. Alba and Spadaro looked at one another, Spadaro with an indescribable expression of fear and doubt, and Alba with gaping eyes; then she turned away. At last, Santa Croce said, "Fine. I will do it."

Soria sank back, wiped the sweat from his forehead, and Santa Croce added: "You will drive in and then get out like the others. I will go on ahead and wait for you. Once you have gotten out, follow me immediately. I hope I can get you through without your being recognized. I will tell your chauffeur where to pick you up."

He leaned over to the chauffeur, whispered something, then advanced alongside the automobiles. Meanwhile, the entire procession inched forward again, halting twice before the Sorias entered the palace grounds. Spadaro kept walking next to their car. However, no one spoke, not even during the delays, nor did the three of them so much as exchange glances; they merely stared wordlessly into space. Santa Croce was standing at the entrance. Father and daughter got out simultaneously with the occupants of two or three other automobiles, and Santa Croce turned around. The Sorias promptly walked over to him and followed him, with Spadaro half a step behind them.

First, they entered a pale gray staircase, which went up two very lofty landings; then they passed through a multitude of other people ascending a carpeted stairway with conspicuously low steps, flanked left and right by lackeys in gold liveries. Rising in pairs, candelabras with clusters of hearts towered alongside the stairway. One flight up, while the stream of the queen's guests turned left, Santa Croce turned right, opening a high door. They stepped into an utterly deserted, richly appointed room, walked across it, and then three or four other deserted rooms. Huge depictions of fights and battles hung on the walls. The footsteps echoed through the space. Santa Croce opened and Spadaro closed the doors. The air still smelled of the pigments of the restored paintings. The spurs of the guardsmen jingled.

Santa Croce was about to open another door when Soria rapidly caught up with him and placed his hand on the officer's arm.

"One moment!" he said. "I have not yet thanked you for seeing us out. Signor della Santa Croce. I thank you very sincerely. You have saved us from an *éclat*, and I shall be forever in your debt. But you still owe us an explanation, which you did not wish to give us earlier. I must ask you for this explanation before we leave you."

179

"Signor di Soria," said Santa Croce, "this is really not the suitable place either." And he put his hand on the knob again.

"But it *is*," said Soria, holding him back.

"I cannot assume," said Santa Croce, "that you wish to be seen here, aside from the fact that I myself—"

"I am asking you," cried Soria, "for an explanation, Signor della Santa Croce!"

The officer's hand slid from the door knob, he turned around and looked at Soria. "Would it not," he said, "be better if you simply asked your daughter?"

"My daughter?"

"Yes."

"I haven't the foggiest idea of what she ought to know about the incomprehensible steps taken by the Comptroller of the Queen's Household."

"She may not know about these steps, but she must know the reasons."

Soria looked at Alba, and Alba glanced blankly now at her father, now at Santa Croce. "I really do not know," she said, "what you mean, Signor della Santa Croce. You will simply have to make up your mind to tell us."

Santa Croce cast another brief, peculiar glance at her, then turned back to Soria. "Fine," he said, "if you absolutely have to know—for I assume you really do not know. . . . The company your daughter keeps makes it impossible for her to be received by the Queen."

Soria, more dumbstruck than indignant, took a step backward. "What are you talking about? The company? What company? I never permit my daughter out of my sight."

"But evidently without realizing what goes on within your sight. Did you not make the acquaintance of two

180

so-called gentlemen, one of whom is named Henrikstein, the other, allegedly, Count Fortescue?"

"Yes, of course! We know them both quite well, and
we have known them for some time now."

"How long?"

"For two or three months."

"Well, Fortescue is a cardsharp. . . . "

"A what?"

"A cardsharp, and his name isn't even Fortescue, it is
Maltravers. Now that by itself would have been no
reason for the Comptroller to take the steps he has
taken. One cannot always know what the people one
encounters are in reality, and one is not responsible for
temporary acquaintanceships. But Fortescue or Maltravers is also a pimp, and one cannot assume that he
does not have his reasons for spending so much time
with your daughter."

"What are you driving at?" cried Soria. "Besides, I
don't believe this whole story anyhow! Do you know
Fortescue? No? Then how can you claim such things
about him? And what do you mean he spent so much
time with Alba? If I recall correctly, he has always
spoken to her only superficially and never for more
than a few minutes."

"That may be true of him," said Santa Croce, "but
what about that Herr Henrikstein? To be sure, the
function he was to perform with Signorina di Soria has,
to my knowledge, no official designation."

The Sorias and Spadaro turned as white as the wall.
"What does that mean?" cried Soria.

"It means," said Santa Croce, "what it means, Signor
di Soria. I regret that you must learn about it on such
an untimely occasion."

"Sir," yelled Soria, "how do you fancy you know all
this?"

"That," said Santa Croce, "I am not empowered to inform you. But you may, in any case, assume that the Comptroller of the Queen's Household would not have ordered me to give you such a serious explanation if he were not convinced that the circumstances are true. An investigation was undertaken, and the findings confirmed the truth of what you have just heard. I cannot tell you more than that. If you seek confirmation yourself, please ask Messrs. Fortescue and Henrikstein—or even better, your daughter herself."

A deathly hush ensued, accompanied by the remote din of the entering automobiles and the murmuring of the throng on the square of the Quirinal. Spadaro suddenly loped over to the window, halted there, and gazed down. Soria looked at his daughter. "Alba," he finally stuttered, "it is not possible!"

"No," replied the young girl with trembling lips, "it is not possible. I do not know what Henrikstein and the count really are, or what they have done! Could you doubt it, Father? I find Signor della Santa Croce's allusions utterly outrageous! I really knew nothing about all that!"

"You did!" Spadaro suddenly shouted as he abruptly wheeled around. "You *did* know! I simply can't believe that people like them could have associated with you for weeks and months without wanting something from you. You must have noticed that they wanted something. You should have said something! But you said nothing even though you knew all about it! You knew everything! You were in cahoots with them!"

Soria gaped at him dumbfounded, as if the end of the world, which he was normally so enthusiastic about, had really come. "Have you gone crazy?" he shouted. "How dare you talk like that to my daughter?"

"I am telling the truth!" shouted Spadaro.

"I see! Then perhaps you can also explain to us what

182

those two wanted from Alba!"

"It was the other way around. Alba wanted something from them, or rather from Henrikstein!"

"Namely?"

"She carried on with him behind my back!"

"You are out of your mind!" shouted Soria, his eyes darting back and forth between Spadaro and his daughter. "When did you supposedly notice that?"

"I didn't notice anything. But it must be true. He is so awfully handsome that she must have fallen in love with him, and I'm sure he doesn't find her repulsive either!"

"But Henrikstein," stammered Alba, "is engaged."

"So are you, but that didn't stop you from cheating on me! And it probably wasn't so unprofitable for Henrikstein!"

Alba gaped dumbstruck at Spadaro, and, after a moment, Soria walked right up to him. "Baron Spadaro," he shouted hoarsely, "do you want me to give you a thorough thrashing?"

Spadaro took a step back.

"Ah," he said in a different voice, "you're an old man and you don't understand these things anymore. Be glad you don't understand. For whatever Alba did to you, you can be certain it's nothing compared with the pain that I feel myself. I haven't got the slightest reason to doubt the information that the Comptroller has gathered. When such an institution reaches such a momentous decision as not allowing Alba to be presented to the Queen, then," he said, stressing each word individually, "the decision must be more than well founded. Santa Croce is right. It would be impossible to doubt it."

"And you would rather," Alba stammered, "doubt me?"

"I no longer doubt," said Spadaro. "I know that you

183

have deceived me! You've made me boundlessly unhappy. But I don't hold you responsible. . . . "

"It's not true," cried Alba, with tears in her eyes.

"It *is* true!" Spadaro yelled at her. He yanked the
gauntlet off his left hand, pulled a ring from his finger,
and tossed it on the windowsill. Then, calming down,
he said: "Naturally, I am restoring your freedom,
which you have already taken anyway, but I will forgo
settling accounts with you. I do not want to add to your
shame. For there would be infinitely more love remaining on my side than yours—if you ever really did love
me. Actually, how could you have really loved me? I'm
poor, I have no rank worth mentioning, I'm mediocre
in every respect. Above all, I'm a man of honor. But
Henrikstein probably has all the magic that a handsome and unscrupulous man exerts. It is very under-
standable that you fell in love with him. Women always
fall for such men. It was predictable that you would
lose your head. Those two men, the count and the
other one, must have simply banked on it. Apparently,
they *did* bank on it. You can't help doing what you did.
How can a woman help what she does! And Henrikstein can't help the fact that you got to like him, even if
you didn't heed yourself. But he *can* help making an
unspeakably low business of the affection he inspires.
If he had had only one spark of conscience, he would
have realized how miserable he would make you and
me. But he had no conscience. And I am going to hold
him responsible for that. I will do so in a way that will
make it impossible for him to continue practicing his
dreadful trade. And I will make him pay totally for
what he has stolen from me. I will crush that adder
underfoot, that villain, that animal!"

He had again talked himself more and more into
blind fury. Now he picked up his sword and hurried toward the exit, taking long strides. The Sorias had been

184

listening speechlessly. As he left, Alba stretched her arms out toward him. "Oh," she cried, "this is madness! None of it's true! He is as innocent as I am! Where are you going? What do you intend to do?"

But he was no longer listening to her. He yanked the door open and slammed it behind him. The young girl wanted to hurry after him, but Santa Croce held her back, and a moment later, she dropped her hands. For a few seconds, they all stood motionless.

"The poor boy!" said Santa Croce finally. "It's cut him to the quick! But he had to return the ring to you. Otherwise, his whole career would have been impossible."

"Signor della Santa Croce," Alba stammered, "I don't feel so very well. Please get us out of here!"

"I was about to suggest it myself," said Santa Croce, opening the door. The Sorias followed him, Alba trying to stifle a sob, and Soria gaping, gesticulating, murmuring, like old people who have suffered a shock.

The ring remained lying on the sill.

They passed through another series of empty rooms. Suddenly they heard voices and footsteps of many people. The doors of a gallery through which they hurried opened into a vast ballroom. People kept entering, and young girls in white, pink, or light blue gowns were curtsying all the way down to the floor in front of someone whom the Sorias could not see. A vague flickering of jewels, medals, and uniforms filled the air.

The three hurried past.

Soon Santa Croce and the Sorias turned left again, and, passing through two vestibules and a short corridor, they reached a service stairway. Downstairs, there was another corridor, and then a door leading to the outside.

The doorway offered a view of the slopes of the Pin-

185

cio, and the Soria automobile was waiting outside. Montalto was standing next to the car.

"Please," said Santa Croce, pointing to the car. Soria, murmuring a few words and nodding his head, hurried past him.

When the Sorias came out, Montalto walked toward them.

"To my enormous sorrow," he told Soria, "I have heard what has happened. Where is Spadaro?"

Soria only made a vague, absentminded gesture.

"I thought so," said Montalto. "But I do not believe there is any truth to that story. If he has withdrawn, then that is his business. In any case, I am at your disposal. I consider it my duty to do so, for I am convinced that Alba is innocent. I am prepared to commit myself fully to restoring her reputation. May I ask you for your daughter's hand."

Alba already had one foot on the running board of the car. Upon hearing Montalto's last few words, she turned around. "Count," she said, "I do not understand what you are doing here so suddenly, or why you are here. Nor do I understand what could induce you to take Spadaro's place. My only wish is to see you as little as him. Please leave us. And I hope that I will never run into you again, Count Montalto!"

And she stepped into the car, fell into her seat, and burst into uncontrolled tears.

FIFTEEN

Henrikstein's fight with Jack Joyce was scheduled for around four P.M. But it was almost five before Henrikstein entered the ring.

First, Joyce had to box against two other sparring partners, who, counter to all expectation, had resisted so tenaciously that it had taken the champion a long time to wipe them out. As a result, Henrikstein had to start one hour late.

The ring was set up outdoors, in the open fields near the English Cemetery. A huge throng of spectators had gathered.

When Henrikstein climbed through the ropes, he told himself that his mood was very different from his last bouts in Paris, when he had been certain of losing and being led, reeling, from the ring. Indeed, his feelings were incomparably better than at his matches before his time in Paris. In earlier days, even when he had regularly expected victory, a fight had never been more for him than a professional matter, as straightforward as anything done for hire. But now, he felt free of that, even though he was nervous and telling himself how much depended on this match, and even though he wanted to return to his profession. He no longer felt crushed by professional considerations. He was excited but unabashed. The young gentleman created by Maltravers had grown stronger in Henrikstein than the has-been. Indeed, he could really have been a young gentleman who enjoyed boxing in public, and who, relaxed and carefree, would have been superior to the professionals, had he also been as tough and skillful as they. Now he was both at once. Maltravers was primarily responsible for that. The count had apparently not intended to do so, but when Henrikstein stood up there in the ring, sliding his hands into the gloves, he suddenly felt as if the count *had* wanted it, and as if he, the count's creature, whom Maltravers had fashioned without ever laying hands on him, had to prove himself in front of the entire populace. Henrikstein glanced down at the spectators. There were thousands. The restless surging and roaring of the crowd filled the entire surrounding field. It was almost like an outdoor feast, a popular celebration on a meadow, when the strongest young men were to fight one another. He felt deeply that he himself came from these common people and also that the man who was not from this background had raised him above it. It was as if the populace were meant to see what sort of man it could bring forth, and how strong he was.

For the strength inherent in the populace is, in essence, divine; and if the common folk does not really, as the myths claim, descend from the gods, then those who are its gods come from the common folk and from nowhere else. For the gods are not the past, they are the future; and they are not over and done with, they have yet to emerge from the human race. The myths are dreams, but not about what used to be; they are about other things, which have yet to come. Among the girls in the anonymous crowd, there are such with whose batting eyelashes the future Aphrodite is already opening her eyes. With the arms of the farmhands, Hercules is already rounding his own arms. If someone furrows his eyebrows, then Zeus may be furrowing his blue eyebrows. And one of the hammers booming in the smithies may already be that of the thunderer. For the races of men and gods have not yet perished; they are still to come, already forming here and there in bits and pieces. And where Henrikstein's shoulder glowed, something like the shoulder of a demigod, towering over the populace, was already glowing; and, like glittering air, the invisibly radiant shapes of promised deities walked in ghostly footprints, entering the scene as Henrikstein climbed into the ring.

Jack Joyce was not all that tall, but he was extraordinarily strong, an Irishman with ginger hair and snowy skin still bearing the red marks of punches from the two sparring partners he had kayoed. Yet he himself had remained quite fresh and was breathing nicely, nor did his face and body show any signs of the hot bloatedness that presages a boxer's fatigue. He had finished off his opponents calmly and prudently. His headguard, the sides of which reached down to his cheeks, lent him a bit of the haughty expression of a man sporting a helmet or a victor's wreath. Clutching the ropes with his gloved fists, he roughed up the soles of his sneakers with sand that had been strewn in one corner, and he then inserted the gumshield into his mouth before the gong rang.

The noisy crowd fell silent all around; there was a

complete hush; the only audible sounds were the far-away rumble of a trolley and very distant churchbells tolling through the celestial space.

At the stroke of the gong, the opponents headed toward one another, shook hands, and then instantly pulled them apart, as customary—but the very next moment, Henrikstein received a heavy left hook, and, in immediate succession, a series of rapid hooks on both sides of his face and chin. He did not hear the roar that promptly ascended from the crowd. The attack had come too quickly for his brain to ratify it. Had his brain done so, he would have been doomed. After all those months of preparation, apparent recovery, and newly found courage, his career had resumed with exactly the same shock with which it had once ended. But he did not feel the shock. His jaw held out, and before his nerves could give way, he automatically stepped back and landed a resounding and, evidently, almost crunching and splintering punch in his opponent's face.

Joyce instantly hit the ground. When he stood up again, his nose was a strangely battered mass, and his mouth and jaw were covered with gushing blood. But still, he pounced on Henrikstein. The air around them quivered with the unprecedented yells of the crowd. Although after this injury, Joyce was useless for the fight against Gonella, his English manager dashed into the ring to yank him out, but could not get his message across in the general raging. Instead, Joyce slugged him in the shoulder, which sent the manager hurtling against the ropes. For several moments, Henrikstein hesitated, merely parrying swings and hooks from the Irishman, who pounded away at him in blind fury. But then at last, Henrikstein rapidly delivered two or three straight punches in his face. The horrible pain caused

190

by the repeated blows made Joyce stagger back again; but just as he seemed about to lunge forward once more, Henrikstein moved in on him, smashing a haymaker into the tip of his chin; several quick hooks then brought him down for good. First, Joyce fell to his knees, then sank half to the left, sprawled full length, and remained lying there.

The entire match had lasted not much longer than a minute.

The raging of the crowd was indescribable. That very same instant, the ring was inundated with shrieking, howling, gesticulating people, who smacked Henrikstein on his back and lifted him on their shoulders, and the thousands of spectators shouted and applauded like crazy.

This went on for almost fifteen minutes. After being lifted and then landing on the shoulders of the people, only to be lifted up over and over again amid peltering applause, Henrikstein at last felt solid ground underfoot, and the throng in the ring began to dissipate. Joyce had been carried away, and the crowd streamed off in all directions. Eventually, aside from Lola, who kept hugging and kissing him, and the trainer Gauntlett, the only people still left were three men with bellies, open vests, and sweaty faces. They were managers.

They badgered him so intensely that he finally told them to come to the Grand Hotel the next afternoon at different times. But then it dawned on him that they might run into Maltravers; so he asked Gauntlett to have them meet him at the bar of the Continental. Meanwhile, Henrikstein quickly changed clothes. Next, he drove Lola and Gauntlett back to town. It was almost six o'clock; he had to dash in order to get to the Soria home on time. Maltravers and Frau von Liebenwein had probably arrived long ago. Henrikstein wondered whether he should tell the count that evening about what had happened or whether he should wait until the next day, once he had a signed contract. . . . Dropping Gauntlett off on Via Nazionale, he quickly but very warmly said goodbye to his trainer, who was planning to return to England that evening. Then he drove Lola home. They had had almost no chance to be alone, and so they decided to meet briefly around seven o'clock. Then he headed toward Via Quattro Fontane. It was only en route that he was overwhelmed with the full awareness of his good fortune.

At the Soria home, the footman motioned him into the salon, but, oddly enough, Henrikstein found neither the count nor Frau von Liebenwein, nor, for that matter, did anyone else come as he waited. After a while, he stepped over to a mirror and looked at himself. He had a small scratch right under his left eye, but that was all. He admitted to himself that he had probably been very lucky in his fight with the Irishman. Joyce, who must have assumed that he had caught him by surprise and would stretch him out on the spot, had positively dashed right into the straight punch that had smashed his nose—and that was his downfall. Henrikstein's victory had been as perfect as only a lucky victory can be. For luck is a component of any victory. Without the favor of the gods, as Maltravers would have put it (he viewed the immortals as something like wealthy relatives, the main line of his family, so to speak), without their grace, there is no victory. They give and take the wreaths, crowns, and diadems. They had once snatched back Henrikstein's wreath. And they had returned it to him. He had won. He had finally won again. The spell was broken.

He left the mirror and sat down on the arm of an easy chair. Eventually, he noticed the silence prevailing

192

throughout the house. All he could hear was a soft, lamenting tone from somewhere, almost gliding, like that of a violin. It sounded like weeping.

He stood up and opened the door to the next room. There was no one there either, but the weeping now seemed closer. He went to the next door, opened it, and found himself facing Soria and Alba.

Alba was lying on a chaise longue, her face buried in her hands. She was crying. She still wore the pale blue gown that she had put on for the reception at the Quirinal. Her broad-rimmed hat was on the floor. Soria was sitting by her side, talking to her. When Henrikstein entered, Soria turned his face toward him.

"My God," said Henrikstein after a moment, "has something happened?"

At the sound of his voice, Alba also raised her head and looked at him. Her eyes were bathed in tears.

Soria slowly got to his feet, walked toward Henrikstein, and halted before him.

"What," he asked, "are you doing here, Herr Henrikstein?"

"Excuse me?" said Henrikstein. "What am I doing here?"

"Yes," said Soria. "Or do you possibly believe that you have not yet completed your job?" And he motioned toward Alba.

Henrikstein gaped blankly at the two of them. At last, he stammered, "What do you mean?"

He wanted to ask why Alba was crying, but he couldn't get the words out.

Soria gazed into his face, almost with an attentive expression, lowered his eyes, then fixed them on Henrikstein's face again. Finally, the baron said: "Leave us! Get out of here!"

"But my God," cried Henrikstein, "won't you tell me

what's happened? Where's the count? Where is Frau von Liebenwein?"

"Those two," said Soria, "have preferred not to show their faces anymore. Could they have neglected to inform you? In any case: leave my home! You are a scoundrel, Herr Henrikstein. I am probably not telling you anything that you do not already know or that others have not already told you often enough. But I am indulging in the satisfaction of telling it to you personally. You are a scoundrel! And if you did not manage to carry out your goals as you planned, then I owe that not to your conscience, but purely to my daughter's character. Nevertheless, your sheer presence in my home has sufficed to destroy our reputation. The Queen refused to receive us, and Spadaro has broken his engagement to Alba. We have become impossible in Rome. Are you satisfied, or would you also like my bank to halt its payments or the ceiling to collapse upon us? Just say the word, Herr Henrikstein, and I do not doubt that you will succeed in bringing about those things too!"

Half an hour later, at the Grand Hotel, Henrikstein pulled up like a madman, dashed up the stairs, and burst into Maltravers's room. Maltravers was not there. But open valises were scattered about the suite, and Frau von Liebenwein was busy packing.

"Where's the count?" Henrikstein snapped.

"Ach," said Frau von Liebenwein, "there you are, my darling boy! Well, what do you say? We're screwed, but royally!"

She used the familiar form with Henrikstein, clearly because of the hopeless situation, nor did she consider it at all necessary to exert any particular restraint on her choice of words.

"Where's the count?" shouted Henrikstein.

"The count?" she asked. "Which one? Which of the

two old con men do you mean? One left Rome after the other raised such a stink that you can smell it all the way to Ostia."

Henrikstein collapsed in a chair.

"Where'd he go?" he moaned.

"Venice," she said, "probably in order to make the Lido a bit less secure now that Rome isn't secure enough for him. And honestly, the instant he scrammed, Spadaro showed up in his dumb uniform and yelled so much that I had to tell him 'Stop yelling at me, Baron; otherwise, I'll have you kicked out on your butt!' Then he showed up again in mufti. I still wouldn't tell him where the count is. But he didn't even want to know. He was looking for you, my boy, and I wouldn't advise you to bump into him. He looked like he wanted to slice your ears off."

"It's not my fault!" cried Henrikstein, leaping up again. "I didn't know anything! I was cheated myself! Why did the count do it?"

"Do what?"

"What? All these base things!"

"He didn't mean to. But he suddenly got a bad case of morals, and that was why everything came out."

"What came out?"

"The whole nasty business!"

"What business?"

"What business!" cried Frau von Liebenwein. "You really don't know a thing, do you!"

"No," shouted Henrikstein, "I don't, but I want to know, for I'm going to call him to account!"

"Listen, my boy," said Frau von Liebenwein, tossing some underwear into a valise. Then she came over to Henrikstein and looked at him. "Are you really that stupid, or are you just putting on an act? Did you really not notice anything, or what is it with you anyway? Just

195

why d'you think the count's been trotting the globe with you? Why d'you think he kept hunting through the filth of Paris until he found you, pulled you out, educated you, dressed you, and introduced you to everybody and their uncle? Why did he invest a heap of money in you, take you around society, running the risk of being kicked out at any moment, and so on and so on? Just so you could take Lola joy-riding in his car and carry on with her in peace and quiet, or what?"

"That's not true!" cried Henrikstein. "I'm engaged to her! I refuse to listen to your unclean remarks! And how do you know about her anyway?"

"You're engaged?" said Frau von Liebenwein, gazing askance at him. "Honestly? My boy, I'm afraid you're as dumb as my poor Liebenwein. But you can't afford to be dumb without money. And you ain't got none. And you're not gonna get none either. You don't have the knack for it. The count's said so often. He also said you could've married Alba. We wouldn't have been all that dependent on Montalto. But you did nothing of the sort. And finally Montalto pulled his dirty little prank!"

"Montalto?"

"Yes. He sent that letter to the Comptroller of the Queen's Household."

"What letter?"

"Well, the letter."

"What letter?" shouted Henrikstein.

"He just told them what you guys did with Madame Levasseur."

"With who?"

"Madame Levasseur! In Paris! Are you hard of hearing?"

"What," stammered Henrikstein, "did we do with Madame Levasseur, in Paris?"

Frau von Liebenwein looked at him and shook her

196

head. "My goodness," she said, "what a jerk you are! You mean you honestly didn't realize what you did?"

"When?"

"Last winter. With Levasseur's wife!"

"No," stuttered Henrikstein. "What did I . . . what did I do with her?"

"You kissed her. Didn't you?"

"Yes," stammered Henrikstein. "Of course. I mean, unfortunately."

"Well, and why do you think you did it?"

"Why?"

"Yes, why! Idiot!"

"I didn't even want to!" cried Henrikstein. "But the count told me to. So I kissed her."

"There you are."

"Where am I?"

"That was enough—"

"What was enough?—"

"That scene. Levasseur kicked her out."

"Kicked who out?"

"His wife, of course!"

"Why?"

"Why! Because it was grounds for divorce!"

Henrikstein gaped at Frau von Liebenwein. "Did he know about it?" he stammered.

"He was sitting behind the door," cried Frau von Liebenwein, "and watching!"

Henrikstein was speechless. "Was she cheating on him?" he finally stammered.

"Not at all! She made sure not to cheat on him."

"Then why was he sitting behind the door? He was supposed to be out of town. Was he suspicious?"

"He sure was."

"But I had never permitted myself any intimacies with her."

197

"It took you long enough. No one can accuse you of being a daredevil. You needed two months for Lisette Levasseur. With Alba, you did nothing. And as for Lola, you actually got engaged."

"Would you please," Henrikstein jumped up, "stop criticizing my actions! I think I acted a lot more decently than you and the count!"

"Ach," said Frau von Liebenwein, "don't kid yourself. You just didn't know."

"What didn't I know?"

"What you were doing."

"I don't understand!" shouted Henrikstein. "Would you please explain it more clearly! Stop talking in riddles! Who did what, and what part did you play in all this? I want to know! Tell me!"

Frau von Liebenwein tossed a few things around in the suitcase. Finally, she said, "Well, okay, I can tell you. It makes no difference now. It's just incredible that you didn't notice anything. You weren't exactly a man of honor yourself; you used to be a sidewalk chiseler, weren't you? It's amazing how many suckers are still bamboozled by others! But if everyone was like you, there'd be nothing but suckers. Well, my boy, it was very simple. Levasseur wanted to get rid of his wife. But she didn't want to be gotten rid of, except for a very high settlement, and he didn't want to cough up the dough. And he couldn't catch her at anything, 'cause she was as careful as all getout. But then a guy named Gomez brought the count to him, and the count brought you. They figured she'd fall for you, and fall she did! It took you forever to rev up your engine, of course, but you finally did get going; you fooled around with her on the settee, and Levasseur was sitting behind the door with his lawyer and his butler as witnesses, and he said, 'What do you say to that, gentlemen? Just look at the way my wife's carrying on.' He kicked her out without a settlement, and the count pocketed a nice round sum for bringing you, and then he took you to Rome."

"Why?" cried Henrikstein.

"Because he was supposed to pull off the same business with the Sorias. Montalto—"

"No," shouted Henrikstein, "why did he receive the money?"

"Because Levasseur's wife wouldn't give him a divorce. The count set you up, damn it! Don't you understand?"

"And that's what he got the money for?"

"He wouldn't do it for free! Why, he went to a lot of trouble and expense. He had to dress you decently, live with you at the Claridge, and teach you manners, before he could introduce you to the Levasseurs."

"I could have met them without him!" Henrikstein screamed.

"My poor boy," said Frau von Liebenwein, "you don't believe that for an instant! What were you really? A guy who let others beat the hell out of him for a couple of francs; you cut dogs from their leashes, and conned suckers on the street. You don't really believe you would have met the Levasseurs."

"I didn't even want to!"

"But you were supposed to. Levasseur was obviously no man of honor. But there was still a huge difference between you two men of honor. There are just as many distinctions among indecent folk as among decent folk—that is to say, none at all. But people imagine there are differences all the same. Or do you believe anyone could have used you for anything in the state you were in? You were totally useless. You know you were. No one even noticed you. You're certainly an attractive guy. But there are so many locksmith appren-

tices, baker's assistants, and peasant boys who are just
as pretty as you or almost, and they won't get any
further than you'd 've gotten if the count hadn't pulled
you out of the gutter where you were stuck, and you
were so encrusted with filth that you were practically
invisible. Except the count did see you. He always had
a sharp eye—you gotta hand it to him. But other
people don't have an eye. They see nothing without
packaging. They allow themselves to be taken in by
gigolos, while the nicest guys go to pot in the gutter just
because they don't have a collar to their name. A man's
gotta have a collar; that's what it's all about. But you
didn't have a collar. So the count readjusted you a little,
and that Levasseur woman, who previously would've
overlooked you like a louse, suddenly thought: Hey,
what a pretty boy! And that's what the count got his
money for. And then he went to Rome with you. You
see, Count Montalto didn't like the fact that Alba Soria
wanted to marry that Spadaro; Montalto wanted to
marry her himself, because she's loaded. So they
brought you into the picture, to turn her head and
somehow compromise her, so Spadaro would ditch
her, and Montalto would offer to marry her. But you
didn't turn her head, and Montalto got impatient and
asked the count what was wrong. The count kept saying he'd pull it off and get you to make an impression
on Alba. But all at once he said he wouldn't pull it off
after all, he'd changed his mind. Fine, said Montalto,
then he'd pull it off himself and do something nasty.
And that's exactly what he did. He sent a letter to the
Comptroller of the Queen's Household; he simply
wrote that Alba Soria was already compromised because she's associated with us for such a long time, and
the queen shouldn't receive her. He said that you and
the count had already helped Levasseur get rid of his

200

wife in Paris, and that the count was a pimp, and you were being kept by him, and Soria's daughter had evidently hired you. So the queen did not receive the Sorias, and Spadaro dumped his fiancée. By the way, is she marrying Montalto?"

Henrikstein had listened to her in a kind of growing numbness, and even when Frau von Liebenwein stopped speaking, he kept gaping at her. But suddenly he wheeled around, grabbed his hat and gloves, and dashed to the door.

"Hey!" cried Frau von Liebenwein. "What's wrong? Where are you going?"

Henrikstein ignored her, but reaching the door, he suddenly halted and whirled around. His face was cadaverous, and his eyes flashed with an unnatural fire.

"Is the count," he gasped, "really on the Lido?"

"Yes," said Frau von Liebenwein. "Why?"

"Where is he staying?"

"At the. . . . " she started but broke off and asked, "What concern is it of yours?"

"Where is he staying?" screamed Henrikstein.

"Why do you want to know?"

"I am going to call him to account!" he shouted. "He is going to pay for cheating me."

"Ach," she cried, "don't be a fool! Didn't *you* cheat people in Paris yourself, and what would you be without him! You've forgotten, haven't you? The only reason you want to get even with him is because the count transformed you with so much toil and trouble; he made you something that you're not, but that you at least think you are! Do you really believe you would have gotten even with anyone in the old days? You'd be better off making sure that Spadaro doesn't step on your toes, do you understand?"

He stared at her, frowning, then his eyes faded, and he looked down at the floor.

"Do you understand me?" she cried.

"I have to talk to him," he stammered.

"What for? He can't help it if Montalto's a fool. We had bad luck, that's all!"

He raised his eyes again. "He disappointed me so terribly," said Henrikstein. "I admired him. I even loved him. Maybe I didn't realize I loved him, but now that I despise him, I know I loved him. I believed he would turn me back into a human being. But all he did was show me that he is as despicable as I am."

"Oh, go on!" said Frau von Liebenwein. "Those are nothing but big words. You were too well off for a while, that's why you're sounding off like that. People can afford to despise someone only if they never do anything despicable themselves. But real life is quite different. You ought to know that yourself."

"The count, " Henrikstein murmured, "said that real life was what he was showing me."

"Well," said Frau von Liebenwein, "and you can see: It's just as shabby as the other kind of life. What do the people who live it get out of it? Nothing—at most, far more disagreeable things than other people. Or do you believe that if your Lola weren't received at court, she'd raise as big a racket as Alba? What's going on with Alba anyway? Is she marrying Montalto?"

"No," said Henrikstein. "She's going back to the convent."

"Very sensible of her," said Frau von Liebenwein. "First of all, I'm delighted that Montalto's not getting her. And secondly: at the convent, she'll at least be rid of men. They're all disgusting. They're dumb, vain, stingy pests, and goodness only knows what else. The count was one of the finest."

202

Henrikstein silently gazed into space. "When," he asked, "did he leave?"

"After dinner. He wanted to take the car, but it wasn't here, of course. He was in a bad mood anyway; he had just received a wire that his friend Gomez had up and died in Paris. That Gomez was a scoundrel. And the count said if Gomez was dead, then he wouldn't live much longer either, and he needed the car. But the car wasn't here. After all, you had to go joy-riding with Miss Lola."

Henrikstein waved her off. "I'll bring him the car," he said.

"You really want to go there?"

"Yes."

Frau von Liebenwein shrugged. "The count," she said, "is staying at the Excelsior. But it won't make any sense carrying on about something that's over and done with. And, unfortunately, it's over and done with forever. But now, just let me pack. I've unpacked enough information for you." And she took a few more things and tossed them into the valise. "Or," she added, "is there anything else you'd like to know?"

Henrikstein held his tongue. "Tell me," he finally said, "what was *your* part in the whole business?"

"My part?" she said. "Nothing. I might have gotten something to do. But things didn't get that far. I was just here because it looks better if a lady's around, so that the two of you wouldn't always sit there alone like a pair of gangsters."

"And," he asked, "where will you be going now?"

"Back to Vienna," she said, "until the scandal's died down a bit."

"Fine," he said, nodding, as if Vienna were just the right place for Frau von Liebenwein. Then he stood there for another moment; at last he said, "Farewell!"

203

"Adieu," said Frau von Liebenwein.

He seemed to be wondering whether to shake hands, but he did not. He turned around, and Frau von Liebenwein waved at him casually. Then he left.

Outside the hotel, he got into the car, drove to Via del Babuino, and explained everything to Lola in a few words. She took it in calmly. "Now," she said, "you're not dependent on anyone. You'll be working again. Don't let the whole thing get to you." He said that in any case he would be away for only a short time and come back very soon. He asked her to start negotiating with the managers in the meantime.

She walked him down and he took her along to the next gas station, where he filled up. Then they kissed, and she waved at him.

SIXTEEN

On the empty nocturnal roads, the automobile developed remarkable speeds. Henrikstein drove through Viterbo, Orvieto, and Chiusi. In the mountains, the Umbrian towns lay moonlit—a boney white, as if built out of bones, like the walls of bones in ossuaries. By twilight, Henrikstein was in Florence. He tanked up, then crossed the Apennines. In Bologna, the heat began. Exhausted and bleary-eyed, Henrikstein raced along the endless glowing roads. He reached Venice toward three P.M.

He crossed the great bridge over the lagoon, then parked the car, rented a motorboat, and, after the boat sidled through the crowded waters with a long, drawn-out signal, as if a dwarf were blowing a silver horn, he docked at the wharf by the Lido somewhat after three. He asked for Maltravers at the Excelsior. The count, he was told, had been there since that morning. While speaking to the desk clerk, Henrikstein saw Maltravers coming down the stairs.

The count walked very slowly, and he was dressed

very carefully, almost flashily. His head was high, but he kept his eyes on the steps in front of him. Then he looked up. When he saw Henrikstein, he smiled and promptly came over to him.

"My dear boy," he said, putting his hand on Henrikstein's shoulder and looking into his eyes, "how nice of you to bring me the car! I was unable to take my leave of you yesterday. So I am all the more delighted to see you again!"

Henrikstein did not reply; he stood there, gazing at him wordlessly.

"I see," said Maltravers, "you would like to speak to me, *nicht wahr?* Come," and he took Henrikstein by the arm, "let us go some place where we will not be disturbed. I was just upstairs. I took forty winks after lunch. I dreamt I was lying in a ship that had thirty-two oars. But you must be tired, *nicht wahr?* Still and all, in this heat, it was probably better to drive by night than by day. How was your trip?"

He took Henrikstein into one of the small salons at the left of the lobby; no one was there at this time. The windows of the room were open. Outside, the afternoon was blinding.

When they entered, Henrikstein withdrew from the count's arm, stepped back, and peered into his face.

"Count," he said, "why did you do it?"

Maltravers settled in an easy chair and lit a cigarette; then he placed the hand holding the cigarette on the arm of the chair. "Apropos," he asked, "did you win yesterday, Dan Holland?"

Henrikstein eyed him in bewilderment. "How do you know about that?" he asked.

"My dear Edgar," said Maltravers, "for a time it was my profession to know everything. I no longer care to practice this calling, and, most recently, I am no longer concerned with anything. But I am very interested in everything concerning you. So did you win, Edgar?"

"Yes," said Henrikstein.

"Well," said Maltravers, "I am delighted. I am truly delighted! You needed this victory. You do want to take up boxing again, do you not? You could, of course, have found something else, but you have nevertheless resolved to go back to your earlier profession. You are probably correct to do so. Originally, I was against the idea. But I realize I was mistaken. However, one should not avoid mistakes. They are meant to make us do what we are destined to do and to keep us from avoiding what we do not want; to make us, who never find an end, achieve completion—even if it is our very own end. . . . But let us forget about that! Let us talk about your victory. I am convinced that it was highly superior and that you must have been admirable. I have always hoped I could witness one of your victories, and now I was not there. But the gods were with you. For a while, I indulged in playing your destiny. But the immortals took it out of my hands again. They too, of course, are not stronger than destiny. No one is. Thetis could not save Achilles; Phol was shot down, and Frigg wept for him in the halls of Fen; Christ died on the cross; and the golden Asir burned to death in the fortress. Still, it is glorious to be loved by the gods, even when they impose misfortune. For it is written that they brought sorrow to their minions. Hyacinth and Admetus had to die, Antinous drowned in the Nile, and Hylas was pulled down by the nymphs into the emerald twilight of the forest pond. Sublimity always brings misfortune, whether in love or in hate. But it is better to be made unhappy by sublimity, than happy by bathos. It is always better to let sublimity prevail, instead of being so low that it can no longer be dangerous. We must love

207

sublimity, unrestrictedly, even if it brings disaster. Otherwise, it will bring disaster simply because we flee it. For it is ineluctable. It comes from the celestial beings. All ineluctable things come from them, doom and beauty, death and love. It is said that love is the most divine thing of all. For the more we try to flee it, the more destructive it becomes. We have examples galore of that. You yourself have experienced it. Had the women who fell in love with you not been afraid of love, they would not have become so unhappy. It would have made no difference to Madame Levasseur whether her husband showed her the door or not, and Alba would not be weeping for Spadaro had she not been afraid to love you, or rather, not just you, but all the men who appealed to her, or someone else, or anybody. For she loved Spadaro only because she feared any other love. He was convenient for her. But that is an altogether different matter. One must be able to love, I realize it. It cannot be skirted. You will, no doubt, say that I should not have brought disaster to Alba or Levasseur's wife. But I did not do so. *They* brought it upon themselves. I played an enormous chance into their hands: you! But they were not up to it. One woman only half-used her opportunity; the other did not use it at all. However, a chance that we let out of our hand is far more destructive than a misfortune that simply ambushes us. I guess I overestimated those women. I should not have done so. I should have realized that they are very ordinary women. Ordinary people are dangerous. They are far more dangerous than people who are out of the ordinary. If you get involved with ordinary people, you are doomed."

"Then why," asked Henrikstein, "did you do it?"

Maltravers shrugged and put out his cigarette. "Perhaps," he said, "because I wanted to. Otherwise, I

208

certainly would not have done it. I do not believe that anything happens that one does not wish to happen. Personality is the only destiny. No other destiny exists.

"But why are you not sitting, Edgar? Do have a seat! You are standing before me almost like a man accused of a crime, although you yourself wanted to accuse me, did you not? Yet you are glad that you are not doing so. For every accusal is also shameful for the accuser. What sense would it make for you to tell me that my actions were base? In fact, they were quite different. One can never judge a person by the people whom he has made unhappy. They are always merely evidence against themselves. One is not responsible for the weaknesses of an adversary. I am responsible for you, but no one else. You did not know what I was getting you to do, and you might tell me that I should not have gotten you to do it. You did everything without knowing what you were doing. But the only thing that counts is what one is. Do you feel that I have disappointed you, Edgar?"

Henrikstein looked away from Maltravers and peered through the window into the flickering of the afternoon. "Yes," he finally said. "You've disappointed me terribly!"

"It is," said Maltravers, "still better that I disappointed you rather than that you disappointed me, Edgar. Everything else is my own business and does not concern you in any way. I must come to terms with it myself. It is difficult enough for me, although it is somehow very easy too. For I sense that despite the loss of my honor, my reputation, and my self-respect, I was ultimately serving a cause that was worth my self-sacrifice. Perhaps you were that cause. Perhaps it was for you that I received an order from destiny to sacrifice myself—and indeed, before I met you, long before—the way noblemen used to receive an order from their kings to sacrifice even their honor to some lofty purpose. Perhaps. For however intelligent one may feel and however crude one may consider destiny, one sees through its intentions as little as one sees through oneself. But still and all, you and I were meant for each other. It is not for us to criticize the ways of providence. In our case, they seem reprehensible enough. But that is purely my problem, not yours. I admit I wanted to make you into something entirely different from what you are, and you obviously thought me a different person from what I actually am—"

"Are you saying," Henrikstein broke in, "that you wanted to make me one of your own?"

"Yes, perhaps," said Maltravers, gazing somewhere into space. "Perhaps I really wanted to."

"I would never," exclaimed Henrikstein, " have gone along with that! You managed to deceive me for a while, but you could never have told me the truth. I would never have participated in your dealings. You ruined lives merely in order to gain a few thousand francs. If you needed money, it would have been better to steal it. I admit I myself cheated people in the streets of Paris. But compared with what you have done, I was earning an honest living. I at least am charged by my conscience. But you are charged by nothing. You have no conscience."

"In point of fact," said Maltravers after an instant, "if someone were to hear us speaking like this, he would not believe that I am one of the peaks in the high mountains of the aristocracy, and that one of the most attractive of men, which you are, could be in as bad a mood as yours at this moment. But that is the way things stand: perhaps I really do have no conscience, although I ought to have nothing but conscience, and

210

you do have a conscience although you are attractive enough not to need one. Perhaps want of conscience is the end of the world, and conscience its beginning. Perhaps there is really a world between us. Perhaps the world, which Soria kept claiming would go under, has actually already gone under, and I am far away, and a new world has ascended, your world, and the sea is still flowing off your hips. My gods and my stars have probably likewise gone down, and yours are ascending. Nothing has remained; everything is new. It is true, I wanted to show you the world and say: 'Take it! It is yours!' But that world no longer exists. Perhaps it is my wealth to no longer be able to give anything; perhaps it is your legacy not to be an heir. I once believed that I had pulled you out of the swamp, but I probably could not even have done that in reality. My task ended too quickly. Others then took over my task, and I was no longer needed. Instead, like that horseman who sank deeper and deeper into the moor, I kept pulling my own hair and sinking deeper and deeper, like that horseman in the nocturnal moor. But you were pulled out by others. You were pulled by the dawn. Like the backs of gigantic fish, the new islands rise from below you and around you, and the foamy waters plunge back down into the sea from the new heights. New gods are lifting the new world, and it is carrying new men, but it no longer carries anyone from the old races of gods and men. There must be some netherworld for me, even though Windhome and Farblue and Hel are gone, the old heavens and the old hells, and the ebony jaws of the gates of death have been yawning open since time immemorial. But you others, you will seek the new gods, new lands, and new women. What should you really have done with the earlier world and with the women of the past! For love as it was is also past, and you have gone the way of a new love. You stuck to your guns. I did not stick to mine, and I was a tremendous danger for you. But you did stick to your guns. You were right, and I was wrong. You did not know what you wanted, and yet you did know, and I did not know. Your gods were gracious to you; mine were no longer gracious to me. What does it say in Scriptures? *Illum oportet crescere, me autem minui.* And that is exactly what happened. You thought you were falling, and you rose, and I thought I was pulling you up, and yet I sank deeper into the depths. Well, I am intimate with the depths, after all. I am old; I have already seen the depth of death and I see it again, just as I have seen the heights of life and no longer see them. The meadows and the forest of the netherworld, the valleys of shadows, the bridges, plated with chased gold foil, spanning the 'noisy river,' the rails and ruts and defiles that sink down—I know where they are. They begin on the dark side of every house and to the north of every village and city, and they lead further down and ever further toward midnight. They are easy to find, and easy is the road that leads downward; one can lie back in the wagon and rest at last, and gentle is the ride between the twilit meadows. I yearn to stop the wagon and go down into the gray meadows, as I so often stopped the wagon and walked through the meadows and lay in the flowers. They need not be yarrows or bluebells or the rustling panicles of the grasses; they can be asphodels. But yours are laurel and life. Tuberoses, they say, have a sweet fragrance, but laurel a bitter one. Give me the scent that numbs the mind and makes me sleepy, but let yourself be urged on to new victories by the pungency of the leaves that no lightning dare strike. For a time, we walked side by side, Edgar, but now I can no longer go where you are

212

going, and you cannot go where I am going. Our ways are parting."

He kept silent for a moment and seemed about to add something, but then all at once, glancing up, beyond Henrikstein, who was sitting with his back to the door, he said: "Ah, already here?"

Henrikstein turned around. Lola was standing in the doorway.

He peered at her in astonishment, then stood up, and Maltravers stood up too, saying: "How are you? I have not had the pleasure for a long time."

She looked a bit pale and drained. Hesitating for an instant in the doorway, she then walked toward Henrikstein.

"What are you doing here?" he asked. "Why are you here?"

But before Lola could speak, Maltravers said: "It is very kind of the young lady to come. She obviously wants to warn you about Spadaro, does she not? He is looking for you."

"Spadaro?"

"Yes."

"But I already knew he was. He came to Frau von Liebenwein twice. He's probably searching for me all over Rome."

"No, he is searching for you all over Venice."

"Here?" cried Henrikstein.

"Indeed. That is to say: for now, he is probably looking only for me. Next he will be looking for you too." And he lit another cigarette.

"Yes," Lola now spoke, "he's here. I came with him."

"You came with him?" cried Henrikstein.

"Not *with* him, but on the same train."

"Why have you come here?"

"Listen," said Lola, "I'll explain. When you left, I be-

213

came afraid for you, because you told me Spadaro was looking for you. So I went to the Grand Hotel, and asked to see Frau von Liebenwein, because I wanted to find out whether he'd been back, and when I came to her room, he was actually there again. He was raging and shouting, because she refused to tell him where you were and where the count was, and Spadaro was so furious that he didn't even notice me—besides, he doesn't know who I am. But when Frau von Liebenwein refused to tell him, he ran down to the desk clerk, and the desk clerk told him that the count had bought a ticket for Venice."

"Oh well," said Maltravers, shrugging. "He would have found out sooner or later. Did Frau von Liebenwein at least tell you where I was?"

"Yes," said Lola. "And she also felt that Edgar should be told that Spadaro is after him. Because she said Spadaro had shouted that he wanted to do something to him. So we went down and learned from the desk clerk that he had told Spadaro where you'd gone. He said that Spadaro had taken off immediately. We asked the clerk when the train was leaving for Venice, and he said, at midnight. Then Frau von Liebenwein said I should take care of everything, because she herself couldn't; she said she was fed up with the whole business and she was returning to Vienna. I went over to the Arizona and played until around midnight, then I suddenly said I didn't feel well and I might not feel any better tomorrow or the next day, so they let me leave. I went straight to the terminal, and Spadaro was really there, and he got into the train. I made sure he didn't see me, and I got in too, and I made sure during the entire trip, but I think that if he *had* seen me, he wouldn't have recognized me anyway—after all, he had paid no attention to me at the hotel. And when we

214

arrived in Venice, Spadaro got out right away, and I lost sight of him. I headed straight here. You've got to leave, Edgar; he's going to track down the count, and once he finds you, he'll do something to you."

A silence ensued, then Maltravers said: "Yes, that is quite possible," and Henrikstein's eyes darted between him and Lola. Finally, Henrikstein said: "But it would be silly of him to do that. I haven't done anything to him."

"Ah," said Maltravers, "people of his ilk cannot control such things. They are far too irrelevant to ignore such an opportunity to grab the limelight. They spend their lives waiting for such a chance. He would certainly do something. He does not even care about Alba or you; all he cares about is himself. Revenge is vanity, nothing else. But you cannot brave it out, that is, I cannot. You must go back to town immediately, take the car, and drive to wherever you like, and I will confront him here."

"Count," said Henrikstein after a moment, "I can think whatever I like about what you've done; I can even say that any fault that is not mine is yours. But I can never allow you to confront him without placing myself between you and him. For if he offends you, I will strike him down. But I have my doubts that you could do it."

"Edgar," Maltravers smiled, "it is very nice of you to want to do that for me. I almost believe that at times you have even cared for me. . . . "

"Oh, count," exclaimed Henrikstein, "if I hadn't liked you so much, I wouldn't have been so horribly disappointed!"

Shrugging, Maltravers tossed his cigarette out the window. "It is over," he finally murmured, "everything is over! It would," he turned back to Henrikstein, "make no sense whatsoever for you to meet Spadaro here. Really: leave it to me. I am afraid that if he sees you, he will not be content with a situation in which your bare fists could carry the day. You've heard it, after all. But *I* probably will only be asked where you are. I either need not tell him, or I can deceive him; I can try to change his mind—above all, I can gain time for you, and we need not presume that he will still be in his present mood once he actually does find you. One cannot rage for weeks on end. A man does not have the energy to carry out such an extreme resolution if he is exhausted by his own overwrought state. It would really be best if you left. Do not worry about me. You should have other worries—above all, other hopes: your plans, your future fights, your feelings for our young friend here. I assume you two are engaged. Yes? Well, then you no longer have the right to jeopardize yourself. From now on, you will live for your future, not for my past. As for me, I need no longer even apologize that my machinations have finally forced you to flee, as it were. For you will not be fleeing. You wanted to leave anyhow, Edgar. . . . You two will now hire a gondola and cross over to Venice, the gondolier will notice that you are in love, and he will make your trip a more festive one than his usual rides. You will glide over calm water, past the white and pink and golden palaces, past the brass domes of the churches and under the echoing bridges. Then you will take your car and drive into the world, into your world. . . . And I do not even have the right to criticize the fact that it will be adorned not with the parks and palaces of the great, but with the back yards of small-scale happiness. . . . Farewell! For it is time, Edgar; you must leave, one way or another, and we shall probably never meet again. But good luck to you, Edgar, and bon voy-

216

age; all the luck and blessings in the world!"

And he put his hand on Henrikstein's shoulder and gazed at him.

Henrikstein gazed back at him, then looked down.

"I'm sorry, count," he finally said. "I'm sorry about you. I never thought I would be sorry to leave you. But I am very sorry."

Maltravers smiled and was about to reply, when all at once he peered anxiously through the door.

Spadaro was striding across the lobby.

He was coming from the entrance and, without looking around, was heading straight for the stairs.

Lola and Henrikstein, standing with their backs to the door, did not see him.

"One moment," said Maltravers. "Please excuse me!" And he strode to the door.

As he entered the lobby, he saw Spadaro stepping into the elevator.

Directly upon his arrival, he must have asked for Maltravers, and the desk clerk must have told him the floor and the room number. He apparently had not indicated that the count was not upstairs. Either the clerk had forgotten that he had seen Maltravers come down, or else a different clerk was on duty now, someone who did not know him.

Maltravers walked through the lobby and up the stairs.

His room was on the third landing, fairly off to the side, at the end of the corridor.

Upon approaching his room, he saw Spadaro, who, having already been inside, was reemerging. The bellboy, who was taking Spadaro, had already passed the count in the hallway.

Maltravers walked up to Spadaro.

"What may I do for you?"

217

"Where," asked Spadaro, "is Henrikstein?"

His voice faltered perceptibly; he did his best to control himself, but he was very pale, his hands were trembling, and Maltravers, looking down pensively, was wondering whether all this was caused by a sleepless night of traveling or simply by his belief that he would now actually have to carry out his threats. The time that had gone by since his decision had apparently not done him much good. No time ever does any good to a decision. . . . "Henrikstein?" the count finally said. "He is not here, Baron Spadaro. Do you wish something from him?"

"Yes!" Spadaro gasped out.

"What is it you wish?"

"Where is he?"

Maltravers shrugged.

"You know," shouted Spadaro, "where he is!"

"It would be simpler," said Maltravers, "if you told me why you are looking for him."

"You know why!" shouted Spadaro. "It's all your fault! You're as big a scoundrel as he is! Where is he, I want to know! Tell me! Don't start hedging or, by God, I'll force you to tell me!" And he raised his right hand, which trembled, as if he had been drinking, and between his fingers, a metallic thing opened toward the count, dark and round, like an eye.

"Aha!" said Maltravers. "Well, if you are threatening me with that, then I must assume that you will not hold back with Henrikstein. Am I correct?"

"Yes!" shouted Spadaro. "You can be sure of it! I'll do it!"

"But why?" asked Maltravers casually, producing a handkerchief, lightly wiping his mouth, and then putting the handkerchief away again. Gazing at Spadaro's agitation, he was convinced that in the end he would never make good the resolution that he had so often uttered. Too much time had already worn by. One shoots a person either right away or never. No, he would not shoot. At least, not shoot Henrikstein. . . .

"Count Fortescue," hissed Spadaro, "or Maltravers or whatever your name may be, don't think you can stall me! Don't imagine that I won't find that scoundrel, even if you refuse to tell me where he is! I'll find him even if I have to go to the ends of the earth!"

"Oh," said Maltravers coolly, "big words, Spadaro, that is all! People always talk like that in such cases. But ultimately they do not keep their promises. Do you truly believe you could kill him?"

"Yes!"

"Then it is at the very least extremely unwise of you to tell me. I need only make a telephone call to Venice, and you will be arrested on the spot. Do you not agree?"

"Perhaps," Spadaro ground his teeth. "Perhaps you'll delay it for a couple of days. But they'll have to release me eventually, and at that moment you'd be right back where you started from. I'll begin looking for that scoundrel again, I'll find him, and I'll shoot him down!"

Maltravers gazed at him pensively. "Really?" he said. "You would really do that?"

"Yes! I swear by the one thing that is still most sacred for me: Alba's life! I swear it!"

I could, thought Maltravers, utterly embarrass him by telling him where to find Henrikstein. He really would not have the courage to kill him. . . .

But he wanted to put an end to things.

He again glanced through the window at the end of the corridor; the dazzling afternoon was pouring in along with the world and the dazzling thing known as life. The days would go on, the way dazzling gods stride across the world, holding the brimming scales of life in each hand. The light was blinding; it was very strong, it was stronger than the darkness; life was more powerful than death, the moment greater than time. For time passes; only the moment is eternal. Everything passes; only life does not pass. But he, Maltravers, was weary of life. Besides, this confrontation had been going on too long for him.

He decided to put an end to it.

"Listen," he said. "Listen, Baron Spadaro! If I were to tell you that nothing that you are so firmly convinced of is true or that Montalto is the real culprit, then I know that you would not believe me anyway. You are determined to foment a tragedy, and tragedies come only from misunderstandings. There is no other kind of tragedy. One can convince people of any truth, but never untruth. That is the reason for every disaster. So let it run its course. But if you are mistaken about the events, then you should at least not be mistaken about the people involved. The fault, which is no fault, is not Henrikstein's; it is mine. He did not seduce Alba; I tried to get him to do so. He was not the one who was paid, *I* took the money. He did not even know that I deceived him, either in this case or other cases. *I* am the man you are seeking. Do with me as you like. I am prepared, Baron Spadaro; I have been prepared for a long, long time!"

Spadaro fired twice. Then the third cartridge jammed in the breech mechanism of the repeating pistol. As if struck, Maltravers staggered against the wall for a moment, but then instantly straightened up. Meanwhile, hotel employees came running over, and two or three guests came dashing out of their rooms. Spadaro was grabbed and the weapon knocked out of his hand.

An assistant manager of the hotel arrived immediately, and in one of the rooms whose doors stood open, someone could be heard telephoning furiously. Maltravers was asked whether he had been hit. No, he said, it was nothing. But he asked to be excused for the moment. While the assistant manager went over to the group of people yelling and gesticulating around Spadaro, pushed them into a room, and tried to hush up the scandal, Maltravers went back along the corridor and down the steps.

He walked slowly, his fingertips occasionally touching the wall, as if he needed support or as if all at once he could no longer see well. He too had grown paler than normal, but he held himself erect and kept walking. He paused for only a moment, pulling out his handkerchief again and inserting it at a specific place under the chest of his shirt.

In the lobby, everything was as usual; no one down here had heard anything of the shots and the tumult. Maltravers stepped through the doorway of the small salon, where Lola and Henrikstein were sitting and talking.

"Come on," he said. "You two really have to leave. It is time."

They stood up and turned back to him. He was leaning against the frame of the door, staring at them peculiarly.

"Hurry," he said. "We have no time to lose. Spadaro can walk in at any moment."

They went over to him, and Maltravers wanted to step aside to let them pass. He moved back, still leaning his hand on the door. But Henrikstein said: "Count! I have changed my mind. I am not leaving you alone. Not now!"

"Ah," cried Maltravers impatiently, "I have not asked

221

your opinion! You are leaving! Here," he said, producing a handful of banknotes (for, despising money, he always carried it loosely in his pockets), "take this!" And he pressed it into Henrikstein's hand. "You will say that it is filthy lucre, but nevertheless you will need it for the time being. If you do not need it, then give it away for all I care. But take it for now and leave!"

"Count—" said Henrikstein, but Maltravers broke in.

"Please go!" he snapped. "You will do what I say! Didn't you hear me?" And he grabbed Henrikstein's arm and pushed him out into the lobby, but leaning on him more than taking him. All at once, the count halted and said abruptly: "Farewell! And God be with you, Edgar!"

Placing his hand on Henrikstein's shoulders, he leaned over and kissed him on both cheeks. Henrikstein felt as if Maltravers were leaning on him very heavily, but the count straightened up again, and, with a sensation that Henrikstein could not explain to himself, he saw that Maltravers had turned very pale and that tiny beads of sweat were emerging on his forehead. "Go now," he ordered. "Stop talking, just go!"

But Henrikstein nevertheless wanted to reply.

"Go!" Maltravers barked at him.

After a moment, in which Henrikstein looked at the count again but could not say anything, he took the young girl by the hand, and they turned and left.

Maltravers halted in the middle of the lobby and watched them go.

He stood erect, and the angel of death came up behind him, halted at his back, and drew himself up to a gigantic height.

He was covered with a thousand eyes, and lightning

darted from the blade of his sword, as from a polished scythe.

When the angel, taking a wide swing, raised his sword, a horizontal bolt of lighting flashed through the lobby, as if coming from the panes of the revolving door, through which Henrikstein and Lola had left and which was still turning. Then the angel struck.

There was a whirr, like the swoop of a sickle in wet grass. First Maltravers sank slowly to his knees, but then he suddenly collapsed, slammed into the floor, and remained lying there.

When the people who had seen him fall hurried over and tried to help him up, they saw that he was dead.

The Eridanos Library

P.O. Box 211, Hygiene, CO 80533.Eridanos Press, Inc.,

This book was printed in December of 1988 by
Il Poligrafico Piemontese P.PM. in Casale Monferrato, Italy.
The Type is Baskerville 12/14.
The paper is Corolla Book 120 grs. for the insides
and Acquerello Bianco 160 grs. for the jacket,
both manufactured by Cartiera Fedrigoni, Verona,
especially for this collection.